1

Jezebel's Daughter

By Jacquelin Thomas

BROWN GIRLS BOOKS

Houston, Texas * Washington, D.C.

Jezebel's Daughter © 2015 by Jacquelin Thomas

Brown Girls Publishing,

LLC www.browngirlspublishing.com

ISBN: 9781625178848 (ebook)

ISBN: 9781625178855 (print)

First Brown Girls Publishing LLC trade printing

Manufactured and Printed in the United States of America

To my wonderful husband who believed in this story from the very beginning. I have been so blessed to have this wonderful man in my life.

Thank you for being so supportive and for your faith in me, but mostly for your faith in the Lord.

Jezebel's Daughter

By Jacquelin Thomas

Prologue

The Beginning ...
February 1968

"She gon' have to go through the labor and birth this child," the midwife said in a low voice. "She pretty far 'long with this one."

"Her daddy has no idea that she's pregnant, Gloria. There is absolutely no way we can go back home with a newborn."

"Anabeth, why in the world did you wait so long to bring her here? You know how this works."

She glanced over her shoulder at her sixteen-year-old daughter, and then back at Gloria. "She had some fancy ideas about marrying the father, but that ain't never gonna happen." Anabeth began pacing back and forth. "This will kill Elias if he finds out."

"She looks to be around thirty weeks, give or take a

week. I can induce labor. Chances are the child will not survive."

"But what if it does?" Anabeth asked. "My daughter has this foolish idea about keeping this child."

"We will tell her that the child is dead," Gloria stated.

"I paid you well. This cannot ever come back to haunt my family." Anabeth's tone was cold and exact.

"Mama ..." Jessie Belle uttered from the small bed. "Is something wrong?"

"See to your daughter while I get everything ready," Gloria suggested. "I'm gonna put the medication in the IV."

"Promise me," Anabeth insisted, grasping Gloria's arm firmly. "Regardless of what happens tonight, my daughter and I were never here." Her voice was stern with no vestige of sympathy in its hardness. "This can never be traced back to me or my daughter."

"I give you my word."

"Mama, I can't have no abortion," Jessie Belle's voice traveled across the room to where they were standing. "I want my baby."

"Jessie Belle, we already talked about this," her mother stated, her shoes drumming a steady rhythm across the wood floor. "There won't be no abortion, though."

The girl tried to sit up, but her mother stopped her.

"Lay down. You gonna have to birth this child. The midwife said that you dilated. Labor will be starting any time now."

"It's too soon," Jessie Belle whimpered. "The baby…"

"Shhh …the Lord's will be done," her mother said, spacing the words out evenly.

She wiped away her daughter's tears before walking away from the bed muttering, "Thank God your daddy is out of town. He won't be wondering why we ain't home by now."

Her arms loaded with towels, Gloria walked briskly back into the room saying, "It's gon' be a long night, so we best get on with it."

Anabeth sighed in exasperation. "I just want this over with."

****

The End…
June 1999

Sneaking into this massive house had been easier than she initially thought.

Hidden in the shadows from view, she had watched as Jessie Belle Deveraux gracefully climbed the spiral staircase almost as if she were ascending upward to the heavenly realm. Jessie Belle was upstairs in her bedroom with no thought that she was not alone in the house.

There is only one place for a woman like you and it is certainly not heaven. The thought burned, filling her mind with venom.

She hated Jessie Belle with her entire being and was here to put an end to the woman's reign of terror, finally. She eased out of the dark corner, pausing briefly to survey her elegant surroundings. Decorating this place must have cost thousands of dollars.

Jessie Belle did not deserve to live like a queen. All of this—everything the woman owned had been acquired through the pain of others. Well, it was time for Jessie Belle Deveraux to pay for her sins.

Her throat was sandpaper dry, her body trembled and began to quake nervously as she quietly made her way up the stairs. It was too late to back out now. She had come all the way here and she had to follow through with her plan.

It was the only way to make the pain go away. She had waited for this moment a long time. Tonight she would end the ache gnawing at her and begin her life anew.

She could hear Jessie Belle singing in her bedroom and eased the door open, straining to hear the words coming out of her mouth.

Jessie Belle was standing outside on the balcony. It looked like she was expecting a visitor from the way that she was all dressed up.

I need to hurry and get this over with, she thought as a sudden wave of apprehension washed over her.

Without another reflection, she walked stealthily across the carpeted floor and through white French doors.

Jessie Belle turned around, her smile instantly replaced by a look of stark fear.

The next few minutes were a blur.

One minute Jessie Belle was simply standing there on the balcony, and then in the next, she was gone.

Shrouded in black, she stood on the balcony, staring down at the broken body of Jessie Belle on the pavement below. She wanted to hold on to this memory forever.

"Ding dong, the witch is dead," she whispered. "This is the end of Jessie Belle's evil reign."

Chapter 1

Two years later
Brookhaven, Georgia

The mixture of anger and grief coursing through Traynor Deveraux's body threatened to overtake him as he walked out of the funeral home. He shuddered in the wake of his heartache.

His beloved Jessie Belle was gone.

Thirty-one years had passed since the day Traynor first laid eyes on her, eighteen and an ethereal beauty with curly, chocolate brown hair, dark gray eyes and full, sensual lips. Curves in all the right places, and those long legs...Traynor's eyes welled with tears at the memory. Forty-nine years old, and even in death, Jessie Belle still looked like the beautiful angel who stole his heart as soon as his gaze met hers.

Traynor married Jessie Belle just two weeks after meeting her because he believed that God had created her just for him. Like any other couple, they had their share of problems and at one point, Traynor was ready to give up on their marriage, but he decided to stay and try working things out with Jessie Belle.

It angered Traynor that on the very night they were to reunite, someone tried to kill his wife. She had made many enemies over the years—he could not deny this truth, but she had made changes for the better. She was no longer that manipulative, deceitful woman she used to be—she'd repented and rededicated her life to the Lord.

Jessie Belle remained a pillar of strength even after the incident. She did not die that night; instead, she lived longer than predicted by doctors, although robbed of the use of her limbs. They became closer than ever after the accident and Traynor wanted more time with his wife. If they could have thwarted the attempt to harm her, he believed they would have shared many more years together.

Anger burned hotly through his veins and in his heart. There was a time when forgiveness came easily to Traynor, but not this time. In Exodus 21, the scripture mentioned, Thou shalt give life for life, eye for eye, tooth for tooth, hand for hand, foot for foot, burning for burning, wound for wound, stripe for stripe.

It's all up to me, he thought. A life for a life. That's what it must be. A life for a life.

"Traynor …"

He recognized the voice of Mary Ellen Reed, the best friend of his late wife and godmother to his son. Traynor paused in his steps and waited for her to catch up.

"How are you doing?" she asked.

Traynor noted her red-rimmed and puffy eyes. "As well as can be. I suspect you can probably say the same."

"I still can't believe she's gone," Mary Ellen responded softly. "There were so many things I wanted to say to her." She swiped at her watery eyes. "I already miss her so much."

"So do I," he said. "I had to put her wheelchair in the garage. I just couldn't bear looking at it another day." Traynor met her gaze and added, "She should still be here with us."

"When was the last time you ate something?" she asked.

Traynor gave a slight shrug. "To be honest, I don't really remember."

"Why don't we grab something at the restaurant across the street?" Mary Ellen suggested. "You need to keep up your strength."

"There's a lot of food at the house," Traynor stated. "People have been bringing stuff all morning. Why don't you come over there? Holt and his family are home with the kids and Frankie's family," he said, referring to his son and daughter-in-law. "Some of my cousins came in from Louisiana last night, too."

"I'm going to stop by my hotel first and freshen up," she said. "I'll be there shortly."

Traynor walked over to where he had parked his car; opened the door and climbed inside. He glanced up at the funeral home, his eyes filling and then overflowing with tears. He sat there sobbing until no more tears would come, leaving him in the discomfort of his anger and grief.

Father God, I come before You once more brokenhearted and disappointed. I am no stranger to pain and loss, but this is not easy to bear. Lord, I need You to bring Your soothing touch to this grieving family. I need Your strength to make it from this day forward without my wife. Please help me …

****

Reina Cannon read Jessie Belle's obituary online, and then ordered a print edition of the Mayville News. She wanted to preserve a copy in a black box along with other clippings she had collected over the years about Jessie Belle Deveraux.

The death announcement appeared in the newspaper on Saturday after Thanksgiving—two years after someone pushed Jessie Belle over a balcony at her home.

Reina just happened on the obituary by chance. She was looking for Traynor's weekly devotion. The newspaper had given him his own byline shortly after moving to Brookhaven.

Jessie Belle's really gone. She's dead.

The culprit was still at-large.

Reina had been in Jessie Belle's presence a few times, but she was never successful in holding a real conversation with the self-absorbed woman. She recalled how badly she wanted to be a part of Jessie Belle's circle of friends, but could never get close enough. The rejection still smoldered like a lingering fire in her veins, although she tried to bury her emotions deep within.

She glanced over her shoulder at the naked man lying in bed with his eyes closed in a dead sleep. She picked up a large, black leather duffle bag and sat it down on the bed, not at all concerned with waking him up.

Returning her attention to her reflection, Reina frowned at her expression. She ran her fingers through her hair, fluffing the curls. "That's better," she whispered.

It was time for her to make some changes in her life and take control of her own fate. Reina shut down her laptop and packed it into a leather bag. She then began taking clothes out of a dresser, throwing them on the bed.

The man in the bed did not stir.

She pulled out another leather bag and packed quickly, wanting to leave this dreary apartment and her life behind. Reina deserved so much more and she was not going to let anyone keep her from achieving her goals.

When she was done, Reina headed to the door, walking briskly. She paused for only a brief moment to look at the man in the bed. He had not moved and she had no real expectation for him to do so.

Reina walked out of the apartment intent on exchanging her old life for a new one.

During the two-hour drive to Georgia, Reina tried to

sort out her feelings. She was not sure how she felt about Jessie Belle's death. She could not help but admire

Jessie Belle's strong determination to go after whatever she wanted, despite stepping on others who got in the way.

It was a lesson that Reina had learned early in life.

Chapter 2

Inside a suite at the Mayville Hilton, Natalia Winters stared at the photograph of her father. Her heart still ached from the pain of his death.

"Daddy, she's dead," Natalia whispered. "We have waited for this a long time. She's finally paid for blackmailing you in order for Traynor to take control of the church that was built on your blood and sweat."

Her father's suicide was not the only reason why Natalia hated Jessie Belle. She felt cheated out of a life with Holt—Jessie Belle's son was supposed to marry her, but instead he chose Frankie. She had real feelings for Holt and losing him to another woman because of Jessie Belle was unforgivable.

It seemed so appropriate that Jessie Belle had passed away on the day before Thanksgiving. At least, it was appropriate to Natalia; she was very thankful.

"I hope you can rest in peace now that she's gone, Daddy. I want you to know that there is never a day that I don't miss you." Natalia wiped away a lone tear. "I love you."

She put away the photo before walking over to the full-length mirror and eyeing her reflection. Natalia admired the black designer suit that she purchased specifically for Jessie Belle's funeral. She was not attending the home going service out of respect or grief. Natalia was going to the funeral to celebrate the fact that Jessie Belle's reign on earth had finally ended.

The woman had terrorized so many people until something needed to change. Natalia never imagined that after her fall, Jessie Belle would garner so much sympathy.

Even then, she still had people fooled, especially her husband. Poor Traynor.

He had no real idea who he was married to, and Natalia pitied him. She also felt bad for his son. She still had feelings for Holt, although he remained happily married to Frankie. I'm so much prettier, she thought.

At one time, Natalia believed that the only reason Holt married his Afrocentric girlfriend was to rebel against his mother. But they had stayed together for so long that now, he was the father of a son. She had heard that Frankie was pregnant again—this time with twins. He actually seemed happy with his wife. She had no idea why.

Her thoughts returned to Jessie Belle.

The last time Natalia saw her was about a year after the accident. Traynor took over the church founded by his late father-in-law and moved them to Brookhaven, a small town outside of Mayville, Georgia—the place where Jessie Belle had grown up.

Natalia had slipped into the house with the intent of scaring the woman. She did not want Jessie Belle ever feeling safe and secure. She had ruined too many lives.

"I should have killed the witch then," she whispered to the empty suite. "You should have seen her, Daddy. The high and mighty Jessie Belle—she looked so pathetic in that wheelchair."

Natalia recalled how cool the knife had felt in her hands. She remembered the fear in Jessie Belle's eyes and smiled. "She was so scared but tried to hide it. I could see it, though. You should have heard her begging for her life."

Her tear-filled gaze landed on the photograph laying on the bed and she said, "It doesn't matter anymore because Jessie Belle is gone and now you can finally rest in peace, Daddy."

****

The freezing rain had eased to a drizzle. Any amount was too much, as far as Chrissy Barton was concerned. She got into the car and handed a bottle of water to her friend, Sabrina, saying, "I can't believe you're really upset over that crazy woman's death. It's not like the two of you were friends. She pimped you out to men—that's all you were to Jessie Belle. A prostitute."

"That was a long time ago," Sabrina responded without emotion. "We may not have been best friends, but we talked many times over the years. She was the one who helped me get my job at the courthouse."

"She was also the same person who had me beaten up during that conference in Miami," Chrissy uttered. "I know it was her."

Sabrina took a long sip of her water before responding, "None of that would have happened if you hadn't threatened Jessie Belle. Chris, she was always good to Karla and me, but you two butted heads from the very beginning."

Chrissy gave her a sidelong glance. "So you're saying I deserved what happened to me?"

"Not at all," Sabrina replied.

She turned the key in the ignition and backed out of the parking space. Chrissy merged into the flowing traffic, taking the exit on the right to the highway.

Sabrina was right; Chrissy and Jessie Belle clashed from the moment they met. She came to their hotel room shortly after their arrival.

"I trust the suite is to your liking," Jessie Belle stated after they checked into the hotel in Miami.

Chrissy eyed her up and down. She looked up to find Jessie Belle studying her as well.

"Remember what I told you. Carry yourself like ladies and don't forget that you're here to work for me."

"What's wrong with us making a little money on the side?" Chrissy asked. She didn't respond well to people telling her what she could and could not do.

Jessie Belle's gaze stayed on her. "You're on my dime, so it's my time. We're not gonna have a problem, are we?"

"Naw...I was just askin'. That's all."

Jessie Belle picked up Sabrina's hairbrush and began brushing her hair. She continued to watch Chrissy through her reflection in the mirror.

She set the brush on the dresser. "I hope I've made myself clear. You three are here to work for me. When you see me—don't you dare acknowledge me in any way. I can't be associated with y'all. Understand?"

"I guess you think you're too good for us, huh?"

Jessie Belle eyed Chrissy long and hard before saying," I need to get back to my husband. And do nothing to bring attention to yourselves."

Chrissy forced the memory out of her mind because it still angered her. "It's bad enough we have men pimping us—Jessie Belle used us just like they do," she stated. "Only she did it at the Regional Leadership Conference. She was no Christian, that's for sure."

"Jessie Belle didn't turn us out, Chrissy," Sabrina reminded her. "We were turning tricks long before we met her. If you hadn't gotten arrested that night in Miami, things would've turned out differently."

"She wouldn't even bail me out. At least real pimps bail out their women."

"Jessie Belle gave us rules and you didn't follow them, and then you had the nerve to try and blackmail her."

17

"I never should've done that. I should have just gone to the media or something and ruined Jessie Belle's image." Chrissy shrugged in nonchalance. "I still can't believe I let you talk me into going to Georgia for Jessie Belle's funeral."

"Well, I'm glad you decided to come with me," Sabrina admitted. "Although I know how much you despise the woman."

"I figured it might be nice to get out of town for a few days," Chrissy stated. "Besides, I'd like to see her one more time. I was beginning to think that Jessie Belle had nine lives. As far as I'm concerned, she should've died that night she fell over the balcony."

"She didn't just fall, Chris," Sabrina reminded her. "Someone pushed Jessie Belle—they wanted her dead."

"I know," she murmured almost to himself. "She must have done something horrible for someone to try and kill her."

"She may have been a lot of things to a lot of people, but Jessie Belle saved my life and I'm thankful to her. If Karla were still alive, I believe she would feel the same way I do."

"Karla would still be here if she had given up the life."

"Chrissy, it was a combination of things that killed her," Sabrina said. "Drugs, the life, and stage 4 cancer."

She gasped in surprise. "Karla had cancer?"

Sabrina nodded. "I took care of her until she died."

"I had no idea."

"It's not like you kept in touch with us much," Sabrina stated. "After everything that happened in Miami, you up and disappeared on us. I didn't even know you were back in town until last week. And we really haven't had much of a chance to talk."

"I'm sorry about that," Chrissy responded.

"Well, are you ever going to tell me what you did? Where you went?"

"I just needed to get away so I moved to Maryland. From there, I ended up in Philadelphia with this musician...anyway, that's a story for another day. The short of it is that I decided I wanted to move back to Raleigh."

"I'm glad you came back but you still haven't told me why you did."

Chrissy shrugged. "I woke up one morning and realized that I was ready to come home." She left it there, not wanting to discuss the real reason why she came back. She wasn't ready to discuss her past, not even with Sabrina.

Sabrina smiled. "I really missed you."

Smiling, she responded, "I missed you, too."

"I meant what I said. You can stay with me as long as you like."

"Thank you," Chrissy replied. "I didn't want to stay in that shelter another night."

"And I didn't want to make this trip alone, so I really appreciate you coming with me."

"It's the least I can do," Chrissy replied. "No use

holding on to the past." Yet, she was doing just that. It was her past that brought her back to Raleigh.

"I'm glad you're saying that. And maybe one day you'll actually forgive Jessie Belle. Because how she had to live the last two years of her life was really awful."

Chrissy didn't say a word. She considered what happened to Jessie Belle as payback for everything that happened in Miami and afterward.

Jessie Belle was everything that Chrissy detested. She was power-hungry, a liar, and a fraud. There was a point in time when she wanted to believe that Jessie Belle was shaped by whatever happened in her formative years, but whatever had happened to her was not an excuse.

Chrissy's life growing up was marred by ugliness, but she refused to treat others unkind because of those experiences. She wanted to be like Sabrina and see nothing but the good in people—she could not.

Her mouth tightened as she took a long look at herself in the rear-view mirror. She would never forgive. She would never forget.

****

"Dad, how are you holding up?" Holt inquired, walking into the living room of his parent's home. His father looked as if he had aged overnight. His hair was more salt than pepper and there were lines etched in his forehead that Holt never noticed before.

Traynor glanced up at his son and responded, "I

really miss her, son. I cannot imagine my life without her. Each morning I wake up, I expect to find her lying beside me." A tear slipped from his eyes. "My wife is gone."

He sat down on the sofa beside his father. "I miss her, too."

"I know that your mom made a lot of mistakes but after the accident, she had really turned her life around. This is the time God ordained that she return to Him, but I'm not happy about it. Jessie Belle did not deserve to leave this life so soon."

Holt embraced his father. "She's free now, Dad. That wheelchair no longer binds Mom. You know how she hated being dependent on someone else. It really bothered Mom that she couldn't do for herself."

Traynor nodded in agreement. "I know. I just want her back here with me. It's a selfish thought, but it's the way I feel. Right now, I'm angry and disappointed in God. I believed that He would grant your mother and me a long life together. We wanted to see your children grow up and have families of their own."

"I choose to believe that she is now looking over all of us, Dad," Holt stated. "It gives me comfort."

Traynor wiped at his eyes.

"It's almost time for us to leave for the church," Holt announced after a quick glance to his watch.

Traynor's gaze slowly traveled the room. "I can't see living here without Jessie Belle," he said softly.

"I was going to talk to you about this later, but I'll mention it now. Frankie and I would like you to come home with us for a little while. We think it will do you some good to get away. You may want to consider moving back to North Carolina."

Without hesitation, Traynor said, "I'll give it some thought." Traynor rose to his feet and slipped on his suit jacket. "Let's go say our final goodbyes to your mother."

Frankie was waiting for them in the foyer and she quickly embraced Traynor.

"I'm going to be okay," he assured her. "I grieve for my wife, but I know that she is in a better place."

"We will all miss her."

"It warms my heart that you were able to see past her faults, Frankie. I know that she wasn't always so kind to you."

Frankie shook her head. "None of that matters now," she said.

Traynor walked out of the house, followed by Holt and his wife. Frankie's parents exited behind them with the children.

He glanced back at the house. Traynor was not sure he could continue living in the house he shared with Jessie Belle. He felt her absence intensely. He had no real idea what his next steps where going to be. In this very moment, it was a challenge for Traynor to even attempt to think beyond today.

In the black stretch limo that would transport them to Mayville where the church was located, he leaned back against the seat and closed his eyes, remembering how beautiful and peaceful Jessie Belle looked the day she transitioned from life to eternity.

Traynor recalled how he whispered in her ear, "I've never met anyone like you."

It was true. He had never known a woman such as his wife, but he loved her deeply and truly. He knew in his heart that he would never love another in the way that he loved Jessie Belle.

Another thought crossed his mind—a promise. He made Jessie Belle a promise on the day she died and he was determined to keep it. Traynor vowed to make the person responsible for putting his wife in that wheelchair pay for the crime against her.

Jessie Belle's death would not go unpunished, he vowed. He vowed to himself and to his wife.

****

Despite the cold November air, the entire town of Mayville seemed to come out for Jessie Belle's funeral service.

"Looks like there is a good mixture of mourners and nosy town folk in attendance," Frankie whispered to her husband as she pulled the folds of her coat together. "I'm sure a lot of these people never even met your mother."

Holt nodded, but did not comment. He would have preferred to have his mother buried in North Carolina, but he understood his father's choice. His maternal great-grandfather built this church; his grandfather pastored here and his father was the current pastor. His grandparents christened his mother at this church, and now she would make her final farewell to the world in this place.

He exited the car first, and then assisted his wife and children. Holt's father was the last one to get out of the limo. Family members gathered outside the sanctuary doors per the instructions of the funeral director.

A few bystanders murmured words of sympathy as they made their way toward the entrance of the church.

"Many people came to pay their respects to Jessie Belle," Traynor murmured.

"That's nice."

"There's Mary Ellen," Frankie announced as she waved to the woman walking briskly toward them.

Mary Ellen reached out, embracing Traynor. "Let's get you inside. I'm sure you'd like a private moment with your wife before the service."

He nodded in gratitude. "Thank you for arranging all of this. Jessie Belle would be pleased."

"I loved her like a sister."

"I know you did," Traynor responded. "Mary Ellen, I hope you know that she loved you, too. In spite of everything that happened between you two, she loved you."

He glanced over his shoulder, his gaze traveling through the crowd. "These people didn't know Jessie Belle—they only know what they heard about her. Deep down, her heart was good."

Mary Ellen smiled and nodded. "There was good in

her."

Traynor straightened his tie. "I'm ready to say my final goodbye to my wife."

He walked inside to the sanctuary, his steps sure and determined, leaving everyone else outside.

"Do you think I should go with him?" Holt asked.

Both Mary Ellen and Frankie shook their heads.

"He needs this time with your mother," Frankie told him. "This is the last time he will see her."

"I don't want to remember her like this," he blurted. Holt had chosen not to view his mother in a casket. During the service, it would remain closed at his request. He wanted to remember the loving and vibrant woman his mother was before the accident.

"I'm worried about him," Frankie said. "He just doesn't seem like himself at all."

"He's grieving," Holt responded. "My parents were very much in love and this is really hard for Dad."

"I think I'm in agreement with Frankie," Mary Ellen interjected. "Something seems off with Traynor. Something more than grief. I just hope that he'll take you up on your offer and go to North Carolina. I don't think he needs to stay in that house all alone right now."

Holt agreed. "The problem is that he's committed to his ministry, so he will most likely stay here for now."

Mary Ellen glanced over her shoulder, and then said, "I'll go check on your father. It's almost time for the service to start." She met her godson's gaze. "Holt, are you sure you don't want to see your mother?"

He nodded. "I don't want to see her in that casket."

"What about you, Frankie?" she asked.

"No," she responded with a shake of her head. "I said my goodbyes the evening she passed away. Like Holt, I really don't want to remember her like this."

Mary Ellen nodded, completely understanding. "I'll get your father. It's time for the service to begin."

Chapter 3

Reina arrived within minutes of Jessie Belle's family and quietly navigated her way toward one of the side doors to the church. She wanted to grab a seat as close to the front as possible.

She was thrilled when she saw that the row behind the seating reserved for the family was available. Reina checked her appearance in a mirror hanging on the wall near the door.

The black hat had a veil made of lace, which covered part of her face—it was for this reason she chose to wear it. She wanted to remain a bit of a mystery for a little while longer

After taking her seat, she glanced around at the people in attendance. She wanted to remember each face present for Jessie Belle's home going service. Reina turned on the wooden bench, noticing the many elderly men of the congregation clothed in full suits and ties, their wives sitting faithfully alongside them.

Traynor Deveraux did not belong in this small town pulpit with dying church members. She could hardly believe that he had given up a congregation of thousands for the likes of this. Reina assumed it was out of his devotion to Jessie Belle's father, the late Reverend Elias Holt, his wife Anabeth, and Jessie Belle—but they were all dead and gone now. It was time for Traynor to get back to the life he was destined for—there was no longer a need for him to stay in Mayville.

Her lips turned up into a tiny smile. Reina had already put a plan in motion to get him back to North Carolina.

It was his destiny.

Reina's eyes traveled toward the front while her mind traveled back to the day she met Jessie Belle.

"Here's someone you definitely need to meet…Jessie Belle Deveraux."

She broke into a huge grin. "I've heard so many wonderful things about you. It's nice to finally meet you." Reina wanted to reach out and embrace the stunning woman standing before her, but Jessie Belle's chilled gaze stopped her.

Jessie Belle awarded her a polite smile without warmth. "You are …?"

"I'm sorry," she sputtered. "I'm Reina Conner."

Jessie Belle's intense stare glided slowly over her face, scrutinizing her. "Have we met before? You look familiar to me."

"We haven't," Reina responded quickly.

"Where are you from?"

"I was born in Georgia," she said, "and raised in Florida."

"I'm from Georgia as well. It's a pleasure to meet you, Reina," Jessie Belle murmured.

"I hear that you just purchased the radio station."

She nodded. "I did. Are you looking for work?"

Reina gave a tiny shake of her head. "I'm a hair stylist. I'm opening my own salon."

Jessie Belle offered a genuine smile at this piece of news. "Good for you. I'd like to see some of your work. I have some girls who work for me and I insist on perfection from head to toe."

Reina reached into her purse and pulled out a business card. "Feel free to come by the salon at any time, or if you'd like … I can bring my portfolio to you."

"I'll be in touch," Jessie Belle told her before moving on to greet some of the other guests in attendance of the women's luncheon.

That day was forever etched in Reina's mind. She had really believed after that one conversation they would become fast friends. She thought she and Jessie Belle had made a strong connection.

At the time, Reina had no idea that the woman she admired had forgotten about her the moment she stepped away.

****

Natalia eyed the woman in the black hat as she took a

seat across from her and behind the family.

She searched her memory, trying to recall when and where she had seen her. After a few moments, she pushed the thought out of her mind, and Natalia turned her attention to the closed coffin surrounded by an array of flowers.

It was hard for her to believe that Jessie Belle had any friends at all. Natalia was intelligent enough to know that half of the people in attendance were here to gloat privately, while some came out of curiosity.

Why did I really come here?

The truth was that Natalia came to gloat, too, but there was more to it. She felt compelled to be here, to bear witness to the end of Jessie Belle's reign. Now that she was gone, people only wanted to focus on the good she had done. It was true that Jessie Belle had turned her life around after the attempt on her life, but it was not enough, as far as Natalia was concerned. She deserved a far more severe punishment.

A thread of guilt snaked down Natalia's spine. Perhaps, she was being too harsh; after all, Jessie Belle had lost the use of her limbs and spent the past couple of years in bed and a wheelchair. It was a cruel ending for a woman as vibrant as she used to be.

Natalia shook off the guilty feeling. She refused to feel anything other than anger toward Jessie Belle.

Being here at the funeral brought back hard memories. Of her mother and her father. Although her parents had adopted her, they had always been a close-knit family and Natalia felt the loss of her parents deeply.

She chewed on the bottom of her lip. There was one thing that made her anxious. Natalia had no idea how Traynor would react upon seeing her. Perhaps in his grief, he would not even notice that she was there.

She truly felt bad for him and Holt. They did not deserve to suffer in this way. Loving Jessie Belle came with a price.

****

"I didn't expect to see so many people here," Chrissy whispered as they walked away from the car, heading toward the church. "Who knew Jessie Belle had any friends?"

"I know you don't believe me, Chris, but she wasn't a bad person really," Sabrina responded in a low voice.

Chrissy sent her a sharp look. "I've told you about looking at life through rose-colored glasses. That woman was a witch and you know it."

Sabrina shook her head. "I don't agree."

"I love that you only see the good in folks," Chrissy uttered. "Let's get inside. I want to find a good spot to sit. Never know what might happen."

"Do you think we'll see anybody we know?" Sabrina asked.

Chrissy shook her head. "We're fine. If we run into anyone from the past—I'm pretty sure they won't acknowledge us."

They made their way into the church and into the sanctuary.

"Let's sit here," Sabrina stated as she adjusted the wool scarf around her neck. She preferred to sit near the exit doors where she could make a quick escape if needed.

"Why do you want to sit all the way back here?"

"I just do," she responded.

Chrissy released a long sigh as she sat down on the fourth to the last row of pews. "I can't see anything way back here."

"There's nothing for you to see," Sabrina responded. "It's a funeral."

Chrissy's eyes searched the sanctuary and stopped on the woman clothed in all black. She nudged Sabrina. "Hey, isn't that the hair stylist from Raleigh? The one who did our hair that time."

Sabrina followed her gaze. "I'm not sure," she said, twisting a bit in her seat. "I can't get a good glimpse of her face because of that hat, but I guess it could be her."

"What was her name?"

Searching her memory, Sabrina uttered, "I think it was Rita ... no ... Reina."

"They must have been good friends apparently," Chrissy responded.

Sabrina glanced over her shoulder. "I keep thinking about the family. I can't imagine what they're going through. This has to be so painful."

Chrissy read the back of the program, and a wave of

disappointment flowed through her when she saw that the casket would remain closed throughout the service at the request of the family.

She had hoped to look upon Jessie Belle's face one final time. Chrissy recalled one of the last times she saw her. It was right before her tragic fall.

Chrissy needed money, so she came to Raleigh to see Jessie Belle.

"Why should I help you?" she asked after Chrissy had made her request. "You were nothing but trouble for me and I don't forgive easily."

"If you don't want your precious husband to know about your little hobby—"

"Honey," Jessie Belle interjected with a short laugh. "That's old news. Traynor knows all about you whores. He has forgiven me and we've moved on. I suggest that it's time for you to do the same. I have an idea. If you need money, why don't you try getting a real job? One that doesn't require you laying on your back."

"Does hubby know that you had someone try to kill me?" Chrissy questioned with a defiant lift of her chin. "I'm pretty sure he doesn't because I recanted my story to save your butt back then. As a matter of fact, I'm still covering for you, so the way I see it—you owe me."

Jessie Belle laughed off Chrissy's words. "You give me way too much credit. I did not try to have you killed, Chrissy. One thing you should know about me is that I don't do anything halfway. I had nothing to do with whatever happened to you. However, let me remind you that you put your own life in jeopardy when you decided to turn tricks on your own."

Jessie Belle moved to leave the living room, but Chrissy blocked her path. "You're lying."

Jessie Belle shook her head. "I'm not lying about anything. It wasn't me." And then, she added, with a smile in her voice, "Why don't you ask Sabrina about that night?"

Chrissy stiffened. Through narrowed eyes she asked, "Are you saying that she's responsible for what happened?"

"I simply suggested that you discuss it with her."

Chrissy could not believe that Jessie Belle would place blame on her friend. Sabrina would never do anything like this to her. Her hands balled into fists. "Sabrina is always saying what a good person you are, but I don't see it. I never have."

Jessie Belle shrugged. "I really don't care what you think of me. I told you a long time ago that you did not want to cross me, but you refused to listen. I was hoping you learned your lesson...by now."

"I'm not afraid of you."

"Then you aren't as smart as I thought." Jessie Belle glanced down at her watch.

"My husband will be here soon, so I need you to leave."

"I'll leave when I get ready."

"You will leave now, Chrissy," Jessie Belle uttered, her eyes darkening in her anger. "If you don't leave my house this instance, I will call the police."

"I'm not done with you, Jessie Belle," Chrissy stated. "I promise you that you will regret this and everything else that you've done."

Jessie Belle laughed harshly. "I'm shivering in my stilettos."

Chrissy fumed as she imagined all kinds of ways that she could pay back Jessie Belle. "The next time I see you—you won't be laughing. You'll be screaming."

"Goodbye, Chrissy."

"This isn't over."

Jessie Belle sent her a sharp glare. "Get out of my house and don't ever come back."

Coming back from her memory, Chrissy glanced over at her friend. "Sabrina, I need to ask you something?"

Whispering, Sabrina asked, "What is it?"

"Did you have something to do with my attack in Miami?" Chrissy asked in a low voice, too.

It took a few moments for the words to come out. "Why would you ask me this?" Sabrina stammered in bewilderment.

"It was something Jessie Belle said to me a while back. I know this is a weird time for me to ask you, but it just came to me."

Sabrina met her gaze. "I had nothing to do with it, but let's talk about it after the funeral, okay?"

She knows something, Chrissy thought, noting the way Sabrina twisted her hands in her lap. She only did that when she was nervous.

Chrissy sat back and didn't say anything else. She just hoped that Sabrina had nothing to do with the attack, because if she did...Chrissy didn't allow herself to finish the thought.

Chapter 4

As the funeral director rolled the casket into the sanctuary, Traynor straightened his tie, the one that Jessie Belle had given him for his birthday two years ago. It was her favorite.

He knew that everyone would be watching him, waiting to witness some sort of reaction, probably. Traynor expected that they wanted a view of his grief.

Losing Jessie Belle was one of the most painful events of his life, but he did not want to share his grief, not even with his family. This was something that he would handle alone. Traynor knew that no one could ever cancel reservations with death—but he wished that he could have somehow delayed Jessie Belle's reservations for a while longer.

Much longer.

"It's time," Mary Ellen announced, putting an end to his thoughts.

Traynor acknowledged with a slight nod, then he

followed Mary Ellen into the foyer of the church. The family was already lined up and when he went to the front of the line, Traynor gestured for Mary Ellen to join him. "You're just as much family as anyone else."

"Thank you," she responded with a smile.

The funeral march.

It was what Traynor called it as they made their way toward the pews reserved for family members of the deceased.

Traynor's steps came to a quick halt when his eyes met Natalia's gaze. For a moment, he debated whether to humiliate her by demanding that she leave.

His lips tightened in anger and his fingers curled into fists. She did not have the right to attend this service. Not after what she had done.

Natalia was the one who pushed his wife over the balcony Traynor was sure of it. He intended to prove it and make sure justice was served.

Their gazes met and held for what seemed like an eternity.

It was Mary Ellen who gently nudged Traynor's elbow. "Now is not the time or place," he heard her say in a soft whisper.

Without a word, Traynor resumed his pace toward the front of the sanctuary. He sat down on the first row, his eyes riveted to the coffin carrying the love of his life. Mary Ellen was right. This was not the time to confront Natalia, but that day would come soon and he would be ready.

****

Natalia released the breath she was holding. She was sure that Traynor was about to have her booted out of the sanctuary. Though she wasn't sure about how he felt, or what he knew, she was still stunned to see such hatred in his eyes. Traynor had always been a kind man with a warm spirit, but not today.

As she pulled the folds of her coat closer together, Natalia could only assume that Jessie Belle had told him about her little visit a year ago. Although she pulled out a knife—it was only to scare her. She had confronted Jessie Belle with what she knew. She also told her that she deserved to be paralyzed.

What she'd done had been cruel, Natalia silently acknowledged, but she been filled with so much hurt and such a strong sense of betrayal, that she wanted to strike back.

Natalia was sure Traynor had to be aware of some of his wife's misdeeds. She never could understand how such an honorable man could love a woman like that.

She glanced around to see if anyone else had noticed the way Traynor reacted to her presence. She relaxed, as the congregation seemed to be engrossed in their own conversations or private thoughts; they were all watching Traynor and Holt.

Her eyes landed on the woman seated across the aisle draped in black funeral garb, and Natalia almost laughed.

It was a bit much, in her opinion, especially since it was clear that the woman was not part of Jessie Belle's family.

Natalia turned her attention to the front as Traynor and Jessie Belle's relatives settled down on pews. Her eyes gazed at the closed stainless steel coffin, a soft mauve color outside with a brushed nickel finish—Traynor spared no expense for the ornately designed casket.

A wooden box or cremation would have been much more fitting for this witch, she thought.

The tiny hairs on the back of her neck stood at attention and made Natalia glance in Traynor's direction.

He was glaring at her.

She had never seen anything other than kindness in his eyes until today. Jessie Belle must have told him something. She had thought the woman would have kept their last visit a secret. Surely, Jessie Belle never would have told him that she'd caused her father's death.

Natalie stared down at her hands.

A wave of relief washed over her when the services finally began. After the burial, she hoped to have a private word with Traynor. They had always gotten along well, so surely he would listen to her.

At least that's what she hoped.

****

Reina had observed the silent exchange between Traynor and the woman across from her with intense interest.

What was that all about?

Traynor did not look happy at all to see this young woman. Curious, Reina was intent on finding out the connection between the two. Perhaps they were lovers and he thought it distasteful that she would brazenly show up at his wife's funeral.

No, that couldn't be it.

Pastor Deveraux had a sterling reputation, but then maybe it was because he knew how to be very discreet.

She stole a peek at the woman again. What was her connection to the Deveraux family?

Turning her attention back to the front row, Reina took note of the young man seated beside Traynor.

Holt Deveraux, the golden child.

She wondered what his life was like, growing up with Jessie Belle as his mother. Did she love him with her entire being? Did she spoil him? Did she want other children?

Reina swallowed hard at those questions.

A woman who desired motherhood, but did not have the patience for it, had raised her. She grew up in poverty, and having to fight off her father's advances. By the time she turned fifteen, Reina had had enough and she left home in search of the life she deserved.

She turned her attention to the elegantly designed coffin with the elaborate drape of red and white roses. There were flowers galore on and surrounding the casket and Reina suspected they came from people all over the country. She believed the arrangements were more so in honor of Traynor than for Jessie Belle. It was just the polite thing to do for someone so well respected.

Throughout the service, Reina studied Traynor and Holt. Through their tears, it was obvious just how much they loved Jessie Belle. Her heart ached for them. She knew firsthand how much it hurt to lose someone you loved. She had lost so much in the thirty-two years she had been in this world.

She shook the thought from her mind, not wanting to think about the misery that had been her life from the day she was born. Now was not the time to dwell on such things. Reina took comfort in the thought that things were finally about to change for her.

Turning her attention back to the services, she had never quite understood why people considered funerals a celebration of life. But sitting here today, she got it. The accolades from the family, Mary Ellen Reed, and a couple of church members would have a person thinking that Jessie Belle had lived life as a saint. Although others who sat in the church may have been fooled, Reina was not. She knew better.

When the services finally ended, Reina rose to her feet along with the rest of the congregation as the pallbearers lined up to take the coffin out of the church. As they slowly made their way past her, she yearned to reach out and touch the casket—to say a final goodbye.

Tears filled her eyes, surprising Reina. She had not expected to feel such a strong emotion where Jessie Belle was concerned. She swiped at her eyes, regained her composure, and waited until after the family walked out before exiting through the side door.

Filled with unexpected feelings, Reina made her way quickly to her car and got inside, her heart racing.

Where was all of this emotion coming from? But she didn't bother to answer the question.

She knew.

Chapter 5

During the short drive over to Traynor and Jessie Belle's, Natalia debated whether to attend the repast. She really did want to talk to Traynor, but she was torn between going to the hotel and curling up with a good book or facing Traynor's wrath. Despite her hatred for Jessie Belle, Natalia truly cared about him and Holt. It was her intention to be there as support and comfort to them.

People from the service had flocked to Traynor's house afterward and when Natalia entered, she was surprised to find him sitting alone in the living room while his guests were in the family room with Holt and Frankie.

Before she could open her mouth to say anything, Traynor pounced on her. "What are you doing here? I would have thought you'd be smart enough to leave after the burial."

Natalia ignored the rancor she heard in his voice. "I

only came here to pay my respects. I know how much you and Holt loved Jessie Belle."

Traynor gestured for her to follow him. She had to walk quickly to keep up as he stomped down the long hall to the study.

"How dare you show your face here after what you've done," he uttered, closing the door so they would not be overheard. "My wife is dead because of you."

Taken aback by his outburst, Natalia uttered, "Excuse me?"

"I know what you did, Natalia, and I want you to know that you are going to pay. If it's the last thing that I do—you will pay for this." His voice was stern and filled with anger.

"I don't know what you think I did, but you're wrong, Pastor Deveraux," she managed to say without stumbling over her words. She had never seem him like this. "I didn't do anything to your wife. In case you've forgotten, I once looked at Jessie Belle like a second mother." It crossed her mind that going back to the hotel, and spending the rest of the afternoon engrossed in a good book would have been the better option.

"I know about your visit, Natalia," Traynor interjected. "You know the one where you decided to bring a knife." He ground the word out between his teeth.

"I only wanted to scare her," Natalia snapped. "Traynor, you have no idea what kind of woman you married; my father is dead because of your wife. She blackmailed my father to get his church for you. I have proof. The merger was a go as long as Holt and I married and as you know, that didn't happen."

"My son should never have been a bargaining chip, Natalia."

"Jessie Belle seemed to think otherwise." She added, "Did you ever wonder why my father just handed over his church to you like that?"

Traynor did not respond; he just glared at her.

"You were as much her victim as my father." Natalia continued, "Jessie Belle is responsible for what happened to her. She made a lot of enemies."

"You tried to kill her."

"I am only guilty of trying to scare her and I make no apologies for my actions. If you intend to pursue this, then I will have no choice but to go public with everything your wife did to me and my family."

"Go ahead. You can't hurt her anymore."

Natalia gave a slight shrug. "No, but I can ensure that everyone will know just what kind of woman Jessie Belle truly was. I'm sure you don't want her memory tarnished because then, you'll risk her sins taking you down with her." She paused to give him time to think about her words. "Traynor, I know that you are grief-stricken and looking for someone to blame, but I am not the one responsible. Your wife is the blame for everything."

"Get out of my house," he said as if the words she'd spoken didn't matter.

"Gladly," Natalia countered. This was not the way

she'd wanted it to go between her and Traynor. But she was not going to back down when Jessie Belle had been the guilty one. "If you're looking for a fight, then I'm more than willing and able to give you one. I have so much information on Jessie Belle that I could write a book."

Holt cracked the door open and stuck his head inside. "Is everything okay in here?"

"Yes," she responded keeping her eyes on Traynor. "I was just saying goodbye to your father."

Natalia made her way toward the door, but Holt blocked her path.

"I'm rather surprised that you came all the way here for my mother's funeral," he told her. "I didn't think you two were on the best of terms."

Natalia stole a peek back at Traynor before responding, "I was just telling your father that it's time to leave the past behind. It doesn't do anyone any good to dredge up bad memories." She shifted her purse from one shoulder to the other. "I need to get going, but I pray God will give you and the rest of your family the strength to endure this trying time."

"Thank you for coming," Holt said.

She walked past him, navigating around guests as she made her way to the front door.

Natalia released a long sigh in frustration when she spied Mary Ellen on the front lawn, intent on blocking her escape. "What do you want?" she inquired.

"I'd like to know why you came here today," Mary

Ellen demanded. She didn't give Natalia a chance to respond. "Natalia, this family is going through enough and they certainly don't need you around here causing trouble."

"I simply came to pay my respects and now I'm leaving."

"Stay away from Traynor and Holt."

She looked Mary Ellen straight in her eyes. "They have nothing to fear from me," Natalia stated. "As long as they leave me alone."

Mary Ellen met her gaze. "What do you mean by that?"

"Exactly what I said."

Mary Ellen studied her for a silent moment. "I knew your father, Natalia and he would be so disappointed in the woman you've become. Petty and bitter."

A wave of anger flowed through her. "My father is dead because of Jessie Belle," she hissed. "If he were still alive, maybe I would be a different person."

"Jessie Belle is gone, Natalia."

She nodded. "And I'm glad about that." Even when Mary Ellen's mouth opened wide, Natalia continued, "Her dying won't bring my father back or make his absence any easier to bear, but it's a start."

Mary Ellen shook her head as if she couldn't believe Natalia's words. "You need to find a way to move on."

"Now I have a reason to do so," Natalia retorted. "Life already seems so much better with Jessie Belle gone."

Mary Ellen stepped to the side. "I see you're leaving so I don't want to detain you any longer."

"I guess I'll see you back in North Carolina."

"With any luck, you won't," Mary Ellen responded. "It's my hope that we never have to cross paths again. I'm not fond of the person I see standing before me."

"In that case, try and have a nice life." Natalia noticed Mary Ellen's jaw tighten.

"I really feel sorry for you."

Natalia laughed. "Well, I simply don't feel anything where you're concerned. You claimed to be a friend of my father's, but you just stood by and allowed Jessie Belle to ruin him." Then she stomped away, never turning back.

It was not until she was in her car that she allowed her tears to fall. She put her key in the ignition, but then noticed the car behind her, blocking her from leaving. She slammed her hand on the steering wheel, turned off the ignition, then leaned back. She was so tired of having to defend herself. She and her father were the victims—not Jessie Belle. The woman was dead and now everyone acted as if she were a saint. Was she truly the only one who could see the real Jessie Belle?

Even from the grave Jessie Belle seemed to have the upper hand.

****

Reina stood in the hallway, pretending to study the

pictures on the wall. But while her eyes took in the photos of Jessie Belle and her family, Reina's ears were focused on the hushed conversation coming from the living room.

"Dad's wrong about Natalia. Now, don't get me wrong. She's a piece of work," Holt stated, "but she's not violent, Mary Ellen."

"I agree. I've known Natalie for a long time. She feels scorned and betrayed, but I don't think she's a killer. Maybe one day, she'll put this behind her."

"I hope so," Holt stated. "She and my mom used to be so close."

"That ended because of you," Mary Ellen responded. "She wanted to marry you."

"That was never going to happen. I have loved Frankie since the day we met. She's the only woman for me."

"I know that, everyone knows that. Even Natalia. And that's what's made her so bitter. But she's not a killer."

Reina stepped away from her eavesdropping and walked out on the front porch. So, Traynor thinks that Natalia had something to do with Jessie Belle's death. Interesting.

From where she stood, Reina watched Natalia open the door to her car and step out. From the looks of it, another vehicle blocked her car and she was unable to leave.

Reina kept her eyes on Natalia, trying to think of all

the ways she might prove useful one day.

She showed no reaction when Natalia turned suddenly, her gaze meeting her own. Reina smiled smoothly, portraying nothing of her interest.

As expected, Natalia turned away, cold-shouldering her.

Reina did not care about the snub; she wasn't trying to be Natalia's friend. There was only one person she cared about right now – and that was Traynor.

She walked back inside the house, her eyes searching for him. This time, she found him inside the dining room chatting with a couple of men.

His daughter-in-law hovered around, trying to get him to eat something.

Reina strolled by the table that held the spread of food that so many had brought over for the repast and then she stood in the corner, tapping her foot impatiently.

It took a few minutes, but finally, Traynor was left alone. She made sure that no one else was going to join them before she stepped over to him. "Pastor Deveraux, I'm so sorry for your loss."

He glanced up at her. "Thank you." Traynor eyed her as if trying to discern if they had ever met and she stayed silent under his scrutiny. "I apologize, but I can't seem to recall if we've ever met. Did you know my wife?"

She nodded slightly. "We weren't friends, but our paths crossed several times in Raleigh. When I read that she had passed away, I was on a business trip in Florida. I wanted to pay my respects before heading back home to

Raleigh."

"You live in Raleigh?"

This time she gave him a full nod. "My name is Reina Cannon, Pastor. Your wife was a lovely woman and she will be deeply missed."

"Yes, she will," Traynor murmured. "I really appreciate your coming all this way."

"I was just a few hours away. I'm glad I was able to be here." Reina gave him a smile. "I'll let you get back to your dinner."

"It's very nice meeting you," he said.

"Same here," she murmured.

She wanted to stay a while longer and talk to Traynor. But then, she felt something. Like she was being watched. She turned, letting her eyes travel across the room.

And there was Frankie, watching her.

It was time to leave. She flashed a smile at Frankie and at Traynor before making her way to the door. Reina had completed what she wanted to do and that was to establish a connection with Traynor.

Now it was time to put the next phase of her plan into action.

****

The woman in the stylish black suit and hat at the church was still on Natalia's mind when she finally backed her car away from Jessie Belle and Traynor's home. She was able to get a better glance at the woman at

Traynor's house, once she had removed the lacy veil from her hat to reveal her face.

Natalia searched her memory, trying to figure out why the woman with the golden brown curls, the exotic gray eyes, and the heart-shaped face seemed so familiar. And then, there was that tiny mole on the woman's lip.

Interesting, Natalia thought as she wondered who the woman could be. She didn't seem to know anyone at the funeral or at Traynor's home. At the funeral, Natalia had watched the way the woman had studied the people in the church. And then, at Traynor's home, Natalia had caught that glimpse of her on the porch where she stood alone.

Who was she?

But then, Natalia's thoughts drifted back to Traynor. The way he had treated her still stung. She had not come to upset the man, but then, Natalia had no idea that Jessie Belle had informed him of her visit....and the knife. It was something she had assumed the woman would keep to herself.

Natalia did not want Traynor to think badly of her. Not that she cared about what others thought, but she had always considered Traynor to be a good man—one like her father.

She wondered if Traynor would ever come to know the type of woman she was, the type of woman his wife was? Or was he determined to make trouble for her?

Natalia certainly hoped not because she wouldn't stand for it. Not even from Traynor.

****

"I was surprised to see your cousin at the funeral. I see Natalia is still acting all high and mighty," Chrissy stated as she and Sabrina entered their hotel room. They decided to skip the drive to the cemetery in favor of grabbing lunch across from where they were staying. "She didn't give you as much as a second look. What's up with that?"

Sabrina shrugged. "Natalia has always been that way so I'm used to it," she responded as if her cousin not acknowledging her didn't matter. She sat down on the edge of her bed and removed her shoes. "It doesn't even bother me anymore."

"She still living in that fancy neighborhood. . . Wakefield Plantation?"

"Yeah," Sabrina responded.

Chrissy snapped her fingers. "I forgot to buy more water. Would you mind grabbing me that one near the phone? I hope the hotel don't charge for it."

Sabrina smiled as she handed the bottle to Chrissy. "I think it's complimentary."

"Thanks."

Chrissy sat on the other bed and unpacked a couple of items from her overnight tote. "That was some home going ceremony for Jessie Belle." Her eyes involuntarily shifted from the tote to Sabrina.

"It was a nice service."

"It was a VIP show of la-de-dah women walking

around trying to catch Pastor Deveraux's eye. I bet half of those women there didn't like Jessie Belle."

"Can't you ever say something nice, Chris?" Sabrina questioned. "I don't remember you being so negative all of the time."

Chrissy did not answer. Instead, she took off her clothes and changed into a pair of sweatpants and a flannel tee shirt. She slipped on a pair of socks to ward off the chill. "I'm turning up the heat a little."

"That's fine. It is a little cold in here," Sabrina stated. She exchanged her dress for a pair of jeans and a turtleneck before she said, "You've changed."

"I have," Chrissy acknowledged. "Isn't this what life is all about? We all change; we are all shaped by our experiences."

"But we shouldn't allow those experiences to define the person we become."

The rational side of Chrissy agreed.

"I thought by this time I would be married with children," Sabrina said. "I could sit around depressed and miserable about that, but I don't."

"Girl, marriage is the last thing on my mind."

Sabrina looked surprised. "You're thirty-two years old; at our age, most women are complaining about their biological clocks ticking away."

"I'm not most women." She shrugged in response. "It seems like women either love men in power or they crave power over a man. It's no longer about love. Turning tricks opened my eyes to the fact that I never want to get married. I don't need the headache."

Sabrina shook her head like she didn't believe her. "Just wait; you'll meet the perfect man one day. One who makes you smile just because. And I'll be sitting on the front row at your wedding."

Chrissy laughed. "If that day ever comes, you will be one of my bridesmaids, but just don't hold your breath. From what I know of men—there are only a select few worth marrying. For now, I'll have to make do with Cuddles."

"You still have that teddy bear?" Sabrina said with surprise in her voice.

"Yeah," she responded. "He's the only gift I was given when I was a child. A social worker gave him to me."

"I remember you told me that," Sabrina said.

Chrissy grabbed a plastic pouch with her toothbrush, toothpaste and deodorant, and then a separate leather bag and she carried both into the bathroom. She closed the door slightly before she opened the small leather bag, pulled out a pill bottle, tapped one into her hand and then tossed it into her mouth. She followed the pill with a glass of water.

"Did you see the woman in the death garb?" she asked when she returned to the bedroom.

"You're terrible." Sabrina playfully shoved Chrissy's shoulder.

"I'm just telling the truth. That woman dressed like that, she was definitely hiding from something."

"Not everyone has something to hide. Besides I thought she looked very stylish."

"Trust me, I know when someone is hiding and we all have stuff we don't want the world to find out about," she responded.

Sabrina shook her head like she didn't agree.

"I don't expect you to understand," Chrissy continued. "Your life was nothing like mine, Sabrina."

"I know," she said softly.

"My own parents didn't want me," Chrissy continued. "When you're abandoned at birth, you just don't see the world the same way that others do."

"I'm sorry."

She shrugged. "I'm okay with it."

They sat pajama style on the bed.

"Well, I don't want you to just be okay with it. I want you to embrace life, and enjoy it."

Chrissy rolled her eyes playfully.

"I don't care what you say." Sabrina laughed.

Chrissy knew that Sabrina was determined to teach her how to have a lust for life. And her friend probably wouldn't take no for an answer. She wasn't going to tell her, but Chrissy really admired her friend's attitude.

"What do you think about going to Mardi Gras next year?" Sabrina asked.

Chrissy blinked a couple of times. "That was a quick change of subject." She laughed. "Sure."

"I love the parades," Sabrina said. "My dad made a chair for me when I was a little girl. It was tall enough for me to sit and watch the elaborate floats, ornate costumes and beads."

"Beads," Chrissy uttered. "It's so interesting how much those things matter to kids and even the adults."

"It was so much fun. I used to sit out there yelling, 'Throw me something, mister!'"

Chrissy laughed. "I can see you doing that." She paused a moment before asking, "Sabrina, how did you end up in the life? You came from a loving family." This was something Chrissy had always wanted to know, but all those years ago, Sabrina never wanted to talk about it and Chrissy had never wanted to push. But it was clear that Sabrina was definitely in a different place now.

"I ended up with the wrong guy," she responded without any hesitation as if she were ready to tell the whole story. "I loved him and I thought he loved me, too. He was in a band—we met when they came to New Orleans to perform. After hanging out with him, he asked me to leave and go to California with him and I did. But once we got there, he wanted me to make money so that he could focus on his music. I was sixteen with no experience and waitressing didn't bring in enough."

"So he pimped you out?" Chrissy asked with shock in her tone.

Sabrina nodded.

"How did you end up Raleigh?"

"He died and I didn't have anywhere else to go. I didn't want to go back home after the way I left, so when my Uncle John invited me to stay with them, I went for it.

But that didn't work out. He was a pastor and he was kind to me, but Natalia and her mother...they were awful, so I left and went back to the streets."

Chrissy shook her head. "Christians are such hypocrites," she uttered in disgust. "All they do is judge others. I may not know the Bible, but I know that God is the only one who should sit in judgment."

"You can't say that about all Christians. There are some true believers."

"But there are more fake ones than anything," Chrissy argued. "Most of my johns claim to be Christians. I tell them that I don't care about that. I only care about the greenbacks they carry in their wallets."

"You are so cynical."

Chrissy shrugged one shoulder. "The world made me this way," she retorted.

"Look around, Chrissy. Not everyone is like that. There is so much beauty in the world."

She looked at Sabrina as if she had grown two heads. "This world is mostly ugly and perverse. But I guess that's a good thing because if it wasn't, then there'd be no need for women like us."

Clutching her pillow, Sabrina said, "I'm done with the life, Chrissy."

"You're really serious about this?"

She nodded. "I'm a child of God and my body is His temple."

Chrissy paused for a moment as if she expected Sabrina to add something. When Sabrina stayed silent,

Chrissy said, "I like the way you said that with a straight face 'cause I know you don't really believe that mess."

"It's the truth," Sabrina said seriously, though she gave Chrissy a smile.

Chrissy shrugged. "If you say so. I know girls that left the life for Jesus and they said the same thing. Few months later, they back on the streets. We can never be completely clean, Sabrina. Not people like us."

Especially not a person like me.

Chrissy was glad when Sabrina didn't say anything else because she didn't want to talk about this anymore either. She had done things that Sabrina didn't know about—things that no one knew.

She had no idea why, but Chrissy's secrets were beginning to weigh on her heavily. She'd been running from them for so long, but was just beginning to realize, there was no escape.

There was just no way to get away from all the things she'd done.

Chapter 6

"I'm glad everybody is finally gone," Traynor uttered. "I didn't want to hear another person telling me how sorry they are for my loss." He sank down on the sofa and picked up one of the accent pillows. "I've told grieving family members the exact same things so many times. It doesn't make a person feel any better."

Holt and Frankie nodded as if they agreed.

Then, Frankie asked, "Do either of you know who the woman was that was dressed in the black suit with that hat and veil?"

"I don't have any idea," Holt responded. "Before I could get around to speaking with her, she was gone."

"I saw her, but I didn't recognize her," Mary Ellen interjected. "I thought maybe she was a relative. I wondered why she didn't sit with the family, though."

"She introduced herself to me," Traynor announced. "Reina Cannon and she's from Raleigh. That's how she knew Jessie Belle."

"Really?" Mary Ellen said, raising her eyebrows. "She came all the way down here for the funeral—were they close friends? I'd never heard Jessie Belle mention her."

"She told me that they were acquaintances," Traynor explained. "Reina said that she was in Florida on business when she heard about Jessie Belle's passing, so she stopped here to pay her respects before heading back to Raleigh."

"That was nice of her," Frankie stated. But then, she added, "Maybe it's just me—I don't attend funerals of passing acquaintances."

"I don't either," Mary Ellen agreed.

"I just feel like there's more to her; like she had another agenda." Frankie shifted in her seat. "First, look at the way she was dressed. She wanted attention with that hat and veil."

Mary Ellen smiled. "Frankie, you have a discerning spirit. I do agree that this woman wanted us to know she was there. The question is why?"

"It doesn't matter," Traynor interjected. "She seems fine. But the one that I had a problem with was Natalia. I wanted to snatch that young woman and send her straight to the pits of hell."

"Dad…" Holt said.

Traynor did not back down and he spoke even stronger this time. "I mean it. I wanted to take her out of this world."

Holt asked, "What happened to forgiveness?"

He paused for just a moment before he answered,

"Some things are harder to forgive than others." He let his words hang in the air for a moment before he added, "I'm going to lay down for a bit."

He pushed himself from the sofa, then with slow steps walked to his bedroom. Silent tears streamed from his eyes when he sat on the edge of his bed in the darkness as he remembered every detail of his last day with Jessie Belle. "Heaven help me," Traynor whispered.

The telephone rang, interrupting his sad thoughts.

Traynor answered it without thinking. "Hello."

"Pastor, this is Larabelle Morgan. I just wanted to check on you. You were on my mind so I wanted to call before I went to bed."

"Thank you, Sister Morgan. I appreciate that."

"I pray your strength in the Lord. Weeping may endure for a night, but Pastor, joy does come in the morning. I'm a living witness."

"Thank you for that," he mumbled.

"God bless you, Pastor."

"Goodnight Sister Morgan."

God bless you. Yeah, He blesses you until He allows someone to hurt the person you love while his or her attackers run free.

Since Jessie Belle's death a week ago, Traynor knew that he was no longer the person he used to be. That was because he'd had plans. He had expected so many of his hopes and dreams for Jessie Belle to come true this year. And his first hope was that Jessie Belle would get better, in spite of her slow decline in health. He believed that

God would answer his prayer for a miracle. Yes, he knew that was asking a lot. But he never put God in a box. Traynor had faith in the impossible.

He gulped several deep breaths of hot air, fighting to calm himself. *You are the God of comfort and the God of righteousness, but I have no comfort—what is righteous about allowing criminals to roam free while their victims suffer?*

Traynor stood, and walked over to the window. It was still evening, so there was much activity going on. Couples strolling, a few kids still outside playing.

Life continued.

Days would come and go, and he'd be left to remember Jessie Belle's life…and her death.

Every time he thought about her death, Traynor would also remember the person responsible for what happened to his wife. Each time he had that thought, he became even more determined to make Natalia pay.

****

Reina hummed softly as she made her way through the hotel lobby and to the elevator. She started slightly when the doors opened to reveal Natalia.

"You were at the funeral," Natalia stated as she stepped off the elevator.

"Yes," Reina responded. "I went there to lend my support to the Deveraux family."

Natalia eyed her from head to toe. "No one can miss

you in this garb." Her lips twisted into a cynical smile. "I haven't seen anyone dress like this since I was a little girl.

In fact, my grandmother wore something like this when my mother died."

The corners of her mouth turned upward as Reina said, "I'm hardly going to stand here and listen to someone wearing last year's platform pumps, fake pearls, and a dress that could stand to be just a tad bit looser…you know, so that panty lines are not showing."

She attempted to move past Natalia, but the petite woman blocked her path as she asked, "How do you know Jessie Belle?"

Reina folded her arms across her chest. "What concern is it to you?" she asked. "From what I could see, you weren't exactly a welcomed guest, so I doubt that you were a friend of hers."

Natalia's expression did not change. "You didn't answer my question."

"And I don't intend to, Natalia," Reina responded. "My connection to Jessie Belle is of no consequence to you."

"You seem to have me at a disadvantage. You are …"

"Reina Cannon."

Natalia's face suddenly went grim. "Miss Cannon, it's important that you understand something. I don't know what your connection is to Jessie Belle and her family and I really don't care. However, it's best that you stay out of my way because you do not want to make an enemy of me."

"Ooh honey, I'm afraid it's already too late," she countered with a short laugh.

Reina gave Natalia a light shove and stepped into the waiting elevator. "You just might want to take your own advice and stay out of my way."

The doors closed before Natalia had a chance to respond.

Who does that little twit think she is? I will eat her alive.

Reina got off on her floor and walked the short distance to her hotel room. She could not wait to change into something more comfortable. She had chosen to wear all of this black along with the hat to get the family's attention along with everyone in attendance.

It worked.

Reina was thrilled with the way everything seemed to be working. If there were no roadblocks along the way, she would soon be a part of the Deveraux family.

****

Chrissy and Sabrina ordered a pizza for dinner. While they waited for it to arrive, they watched a movie on Lifetime.

"That man was crazy," Sabrina said when the movie ended. "He stalked that woman across four states."

"I'm glad I never had to deal with something like that," Chrissy stated.

Sabrina agreed. "God was definitely looking out for

us when we were out there on the streets, girl. I just shudder thinking about the chances we took with our lives."

When the pizza arrived, they settled down at the small table to eat.

"So now that we're here in the hotel, the funeral is over and we don't have anywhere else to be, tell me…who was behind the attack in Miami," Chrissy said after placing two slices of pepperoni pizza on a paper plate.

Sabrina sighed, realized that Chrissy wasn't about to let this go. Actually, it was probably time for the truth.

Sabrina remembered that day well. It was the one and only time she ever bore witness to Jessie Belle's anger— the night Chrissy was arrested.

"I should have you thrown out of one of these windows," Jessie Belle told Sabrina.

Taking a step backward, she asked, "For what? I didn't do anything."

"You brought that greedy whore into my life. Now, I want you to fix it."

"What do you want me to do, Jessie Belle?" Sabrina questioned.

"Find a way to shut her up," she ordered. "I mean it."

"I have a cousin here who could use some money," Karla interjected. "He…uh, likes to beat on women. He could scare her—you know?"

"I don't care what you do," Jessie Belle uttered. "I just want Chrissy out of my life once and for all."

"Sabrina," Chrissy prompted.

"I'm sorry," she murmured as she blinked herself back to the present. "Jessie Belle was angry and she told us that you were a problem and that we needed to find a way to shut you up."

"You were a part of this?"

Sabrina felt awful. She could see the hurt on Chrissy's face and hear it in her tone. "No," she shook her head, "I tried to talk Karla out of it, but she wouldn't listen to me. She called her cousin and he…he beat you up."

Chrissy paused, letting this information sink into her mind. "All this time, you knew this and you never said anything?" She didn't give Sabrina a chance to respond. "You were supposed to be my friend. I ride for you and I thought you felt the same way."

"Girl, you know that we ride for each other," she assured her. "I tried to talk Karla out of calling him, but you two were feuding and she wouldn't change her mind. Chris, please forgive me. I would have told you, but remember, you left town right after that."

"I knew Jessie Belle was behind it," she muttered. "I knew it."

"I'm so sorry, Chris," she apologized again.

She sat with her back straight and her arms folded across her chest. "So you've said."

"Can you please forgive me?" Sabrina asked.

There was quiet for a moment, and then, "I can try," Chrissy stated. "You have always been like a sister to me. I want to believe that you'd never do something like this to me."

"I wouldn't," Sabrina responded softly. "Jessie Belle made us leave on the first flight back to Raleigh. I had no idea that you were even in the hospital until later. After that, Karla and I didn't really talk. We only got close again when she found out that she had cancer."

"Karla better be thankful that she's dead already," Chrissy huffed. "I guess God really don't like ugly 'cause Jessie Belle and Karla tried to get rid of me and they both rotting away in graves."

"Or maybe it's that God's given you a second chance to change your life."

Chrissy shook her head and waved her hands. "Sabrina, I know you not going all holy roller on me. Don't forget, you was all about that life, too." She bit into a slice of pizza.

"I own it, Chris," Sabrina retorted. "I used to be about that life, but not anymore. I gave it up and I've been forgiven of my sins."

Chrissy shrugged. "If you say so."

"It's the truth," Sabrina said. "Despite any sins I've done in the past and any sin I may commit now, God loves me because I'm a Christian. Last Sunday, Pastor Poolee preached on this. In the Bible, the disciples asked Jesus how many times they should forgive their brother who sins against them and Jesus replied seventy times seven."

Chrissy wiped her mouth with a paper napkin and chuckled. "Really?"

Sabrina nodded and ignored her friend's skepticism. "When you are born of God and He looks upon you, all He sees is the righteous Blood of the Lamb that covers you. That's why both Paul and John say that Christians do not sin. While we may do things that are wrong, that sin will never affect our standing in regards to us being God's sons and daughters."

Chrissy frowned as if she were confused. "Who are Paul and John?" she asked as if she expected Sabrina to tell her that they were men they once knew.

"They were disciples of Jesus."

"Oh."

Sabrina kept on, "Chris, the gift of eternal life is free. You can accept it right now—at this very moment."

She shook her head and held up her hand in dismissal. "Girl, God ain't interested in people like you and me."

Sabrina reached for another slice. "That's not true. What's so awesome is that regardless of who we are or how bad we may have been, God still loves us with an awesome love and He wants all of His children to accept the gift of eternal life through faith in His Son."

Skeptical, Chrissy shook her head. "It can't be as easy as you make it sound."

"But it is," Sabrina insisted. "If you confess with your mouth that Jesus is the Son of God, and believe in your heart that God raised Him from the dead, you will be saved."

"Just like that?"

Sabrina nodded. "That's all it takes, Chris."

Chrissy remained silent for a moment. It was amazing to her the way Sabrina was talking. As if she really knew God and knew all of these things about Him. "I can't say I believe in all that, in everything that you're saying." Her gaze traveled over to the Bible on the nightstand. "I've never even opened one of those." She motioned with her chin toward the Bible.

"It doesn't matter what you did before. It's never too late to accept Christ. But keep in mind that tomorrow is promised to no one."

They were both silent for several minutes as they each finished off another slice of pizza. Then, Chrissy said, "So you're really into the church scene now?"

Sabrina nodded. "I love the Lord and I want everything that I do to glorify Him. I even sing in the choir."

Chrissy's eyes widened in surprise. "What? You be up there singing?"

Sabrina laughed. "Yeah, girl. I love it."

"So now that you all saved and everything...you gave up sex, too?"

"I'm celibate." She held out her hand. "This is my purity ring."

Chrissy studied the gold band and chuckled. "That ship has sailed, sweetie. Ain't no purity left."

Sabrina laughed. "You're crazy, but I love you, girl."

Then, it was Sabrina who changed the subject, talking them down memory lane to some of the good times they'd had together.

But while their talk of the past brought many chuckles, memories of her own past haunted Chrissy.

****

Chrissy was still awake long after Sabrina had fallen asleep.

When she'd come back to Raleigh, she was not surprised to find that her friend was no longer turning tricks. But tonight…she was shocked that Sabrina was so serious about church. Then again, maybe she shouldn't have been so surprised. When they were in the life, Sabrina always had a phobia about working anywhere near a church, temple, or any religious building. She was afraid that lightning would strike her or something crazy like that.

It was only because of Sabrina's fear that Chrissy avoided those settings as well since religion had never been a part of her life.

But then again, she never had much of a life period.

Chrissy had a lonely childhood with no one to give her the love and affection that she craved as a young girl. Growing up in a group home, she used to believe that she was unlovable.

That was why she gravitated toward boys, especially those who would pay her compliments in high school. But most times, those short-lived relationships resulted in heartbreak. That was one of the reasons she ended up dropping out of school and working the streets.

There had been a time when she aspired to go to college, but she became too immersed in prostitution. She loved the power and the control that it gave her. Though she did have other dreams. She hoped that one day she would meet a wealthy man who would whisk her away from that life. By the time she turned thirty, though, Chrissy decided that all of those dreams were never coming true and love was not in the plan for her.

She took control of her own life on the streets, only working for a pimp briefly. But after he broke her arm, she left Atlanta and never looked back. After that experience, Chrissy never had any use for working with a pimp or madam – which is one of the reasons why she clashed with Jessie Belle from the moment they met.

But now, it was time to change some things. In February, she would turn thirty-three—she had to make better choices for her life. Though she had a nice little savings set aside, she was reluctant to touch it. Prostitution didn't come with a 401K or a pension. So the first thing she'd have to do if she was going to leave the life was get a job as soon as they returned to Raleigh.

Her mind felt like it was in overdrive with all of these thoughts. Chrissy tossed from one side of the bed to the other. Sleep would not come easy, not with all the decisions she had to make.

Or maybe it wasn't the decisions of the future that were keeping her awake. Maybe it was all the memories of the past that wouldn't allow her to sleep. Maybe it was those memories that would never allow her to escape, no matter where she went, no matter what she tried to do.

She would never be able to get away. And that's what scared Chrissy the most.

****

"Wait, Mary Ellen. . . I've made a decision," Traynor announced the next day, just as she was preparing to leave. "I received an offer from a church in Raleigh a few weeks ago. I'd intended to turn them down, but then we lost Jessie Belle ..." His voice died off.

"Dad," Holt prompted. "Are you reconsidering?"

Traynor nodded. "Yes, I am, son. There is nothing left for me here, so I'm going to take the job in Raleigh at Bright Hope Christian Church. I'll be closer to you, Frankie, and the grandchildren." He was actually looking forward to the birth of his granddaughters in April.

"I had no idea that Pastor Jennings was gone," Mary Ellen stated. "He's been at Bright Hope for almost five years. His uncle was pastor before that."

"I recently heard something about his leaving," Holt interjected. "He resigned a few weeks ago, and then left town without saying anything to his wife or anyone. From what I understand. No one has heard from him since."

"I think I remember him," Traynor said. "He was a real young guy when he took over Bright Hope. He loved to dress in tailored suits with matching shoes, if I remember correctly."

"That's him," Mary Ellen confirmed with a chuckle. "He's nice looking and he knows it. I believe that's why his congregation is largely female."

"I guess that'll change when I get there." Traynor walked over to the fireplace and picked up a photograph. After a few silent seconds, he said, "I love this picture of your mother."

Holt smiled. "So do I. It's one of my favorites."

Mary Ellen gave them both a moment before she said, "I need to get going, I have an early flight out tomorrow morning." She hugged Traynor. "I'm so glad you're coming back to Raleigh."

Next, she embraced her Holt and kissed his cheek. "Love you, sweetie."

She walked out of the house after hugging Frankie and the children.

Traynor stood on the porch waving as she pulled away in her rental. The sun was going down and he was growing wearier by the moment.

Going back into the house, he sat down in the family room and watched a movie. Though Holt and Frankie watched it, too, the animated feature was for his grandson.

Ninety minutes later when the movie ended, Traynor rose to his feet and said, "I'll see y'all in the morning. Time for bed."

"Awwwww ..." his grandson groaned. "I thought we were going to watch two movies."

"We can watch the other movie tomorrow," he said.

"Grandpa's tired."

"C'mon, Junior," Frankie said. "You need to get ready for bed, too. We've all had a busy day today."

Traynor gave his daughter-in-law a grateful smile. He loved his grandson, but right now, he preferred to go into his bedroom and spend the rest of his evening in solitude.

****

"I'm glad we're getting out of here," Chrissy stated. "This place is boring."

"How do you know?" Sabrina inquired. "We haven't been anywhere outside of the church and this hotel."

"That's because there is no place else to go. This town is one exit in and one exit out. I could walk this entire town and not be out of breath when I'm done."

With their hands filled with their overnight bags and purses, they stepped out of the elevator and into the lobby. The moment they did, Chrissy noticed the woman at the front desk and she gestured to Sabrina. "There's the hairdresser."

When they got closer, Sabrina said, "Hello Reina …"

She turned around and eyed the two women standing behind her. "Do I know you?" she asked coolly.

"Jessie Belle brought us to your salon a few years ago," Sabrina replied. "You did our hair because we were traveling to Miami for a conference."

"That was a long time ago," Reina said.

Then, her eyes traveled to Chrissy, when Chrissy said,

"I was a little surprised to see you at the funeral yesterday. I had no idea you and Jessie Belle were so close."

"Well, there's a lot you really don't know about me," Reina retorted. She shook her head. "This town really needs another hotel."

Chrissy rolled her eyes while Sabrina responded, "It's been a while since I last saw you and I just wanted to say hello. Are you still in Raleigh? Because that's where we live, too."

"Yes," she said curtly. Her cutting gaze remained on Chrissy for a moment before Reina added, "I need to get going, but my salon is still in the same location—though, I also have a second shop now. My new one is in North Hills. It's where I am most days." She fingered one of Sabrina's curling tendrils. "Split ends. You should come see me." Then, Reina glanced over at Chrissy. "You should come, too. I'm sure we can give you a better sew-in that will compliment your complexion. That blond hair makes you look washed out."

Sending Reina a sharp look, Chrissy said, "I have a hairstylist and I'm perfectly happy with her. Would love to chat with you longer, but we really need to get on the road."

"You two drove down?" Reina asked as if she were surprised.

"Yeah," Chrissy responded. "Why?"

"I drove here as well." Reina picked up her weekender. "I guess I'll see you on the highway."

"Not if I can help it," Chrissy muttered.

Reina walked out of the lobby in front of them, and Sabrina asked, "Don't you get along with anybody?"

"She's nothing," Chrissy responded. "Do you remember the way she was hanging onto Jessie Belle's every word while we were getting our hair done? She was nothing more than a lapdog."

"I think she wanted to be a part of Jessie Belle's circle," Sabrina said. "Instead I watched Jessie Belle reject her at every turn. I felt bad for her."

"I never wanted Reina to do my hair again. Who knows … she might have shaved me bald for that witch."

Sabrina chuckled. "No surprise there. I can count on one hand the number of people you trust and still have fingers left over."

"Hey, I don't take to folks like that. I have trust issues and for good reason."

"I hope that you still count me among the people you trust," Sabrina said as the two of them slipped into the car.

A couple of seconds ticked by before Chrissy said, "It's in the past. All is forgiven." She slipped on her sunglasses. "It's time we headed home. I don't like driving in the dark."

As they drove back to Raleigh, the car was silent. They didn't even bother to turn on the radio, as both women seemed satisfied to stay inside their own thoughts.

Chrissy couldn't get her mind to focus on just one thought. She went from thoughts of her past to her conversation with Sabrina last night. She couldn't believe how much Sabrina had her thinking about God, especially everything she'd said about God's forgiveness. But it was hard for Chrissy to believe that He would forgive her sins just like that. Especially the sins that she'd committed.

She had always heard that God was angry and judgmental and after all she had done, Chrissy knew that she didn't have a prayer of getting into heaven. No matter how much she scrubbed her body, she never felt clean enough. She was always soiled.

The sad thing was that Sabrina was also soiled—only she chose to believe that she was suddenly free of her sins and would one day see Jesus. Chrissy felt sorry for Sabrina.

Sabrina just didn't know any better. But Chrissy wasn't going to tell her that. Sabrina would have to find out for herself.

Chapter 7

Reina sat in her car and waited for Sabrina and her friend to exit the hotel. She didn't like them, especially the one with the horrible sew-in. She slipped on her sunglasses as soon as she spotted them. Reina vaguely remembered the two women—recalling only that Jessie Belle had brought them to her salon.

At the time, she could not understand how women like them could be a part of Jessie Belle's small circle. What type of work did they perform for her? she had wondered then, and she wondered now.

The two appeared to be in deep conversation while walking over to a black Honda Accord with expensive-looking rims.

A smiled tugged on her lips as Reina waited for them to pull out of the parking lot. She turned the ignition and left the hotel minutes later, merging into the flowing traffic. She turned on her favorite music to make the long drive home much easier to bear.

There would be some questions asked when she returned to Raleigh, but Reina was prepared to answer everything. And then, the situation with her church would straighten itself out. They would have a new pastor.

Traynor Deveraux.

She fully believed that he would accept the position. Now that his wife was gone, Reina had no doubt that he would leave Georgia. His son, Frankie, and grandson lived in Raleigh. So of course now, he'd want to be with his family. And her church was open for him. She'd made sure of that.

She loved when a plan came together.

Reina was exhausted by the time she pulled in the driveway of her home. She did not relish making the drive back to North Carolina—it was a long day for her.

"It's good to be back here," Reina whispered to the empty house as she dropped her suitcase near the staircase. She had been away from home for almost three weeks, though that hadn't been planned. She'd stayed in Florida longer than expected.

As soon as she settled down in her den, the telephone rang and Reina groaned in irritation. Checking the Caller ID, she saw that it was her friend Kate. She loved her dearly, but the woman was a huge gossip.

"Hello, Kate," she said into the receiver.

"When did you get back? I've been calling you all week. I tried your cell and never got an answer. I—"

"What's up?" Reina interjected.

"No one has heard from Pastor Mike," Kate announced. "His wife is really worried about him."

"I'm sure he's fine," Reina said. "He probably just needs some time alone. That's most likely why he resigned so abruptly."

Pastor Michael Jennings was the pastor of the church

she and Kate attended. A couple of weeks ago, he abruptly announced his decision to leave Bright Hope. A few days later, he left town without a word to anyone, including his wife, Charlotte.

The whole church knew that Charlotte and her husband were having marital problems. So to Reina, it was no surprise that Pastor Mike had left his wife behind.

"It's a shame the way he's treating Charlotte," Kate huffed. "The poor thing nearly cried her eyes out."

"For all we know, she drove him away," Reina said, sounding like she was hardly interested. "She was jealous and petty. She couldn't stand to see him talking to a pretty woman."

"You never have anything nice to say about Charlotte. Why don't you like her?"

"I never said I didn't like her," she responded. "I just know how she is and I don't have time or patience for drama."

After a couple of seconds, Kate said, "Well, I know we have to move on and I really hope that we'll be able to get Traynor Deveraux as our new pastor. I have always liked him."

Reina agreed. "I think we have a better chance now that his wife is gone. I don't believe he would've considered our request at all if she were still alive."

"That's so awful that she died," Kate murmured. "I feel so bad for him. He really loved her."

"She was his life," Reina said, as the funeral services played through her mind once again. "I've never seen a man so stricken with grief. My heart ached for him."

"Wait. When did you see Pastor Deveraux?" Kate inquired.

"I attended the funeral for his wife," Reina said as if that was the most natural thing. "I've known them for a long time."

"I didn't know that," Kate said, with surprise in her tone. "So that's where you've been?"

Reina sighed. "If you must know … yes. I was with the family."

"Wow. So, did you ask him about pastoring Bright Hope?"

"Of course not, Kate," Reina snapped. "The man suffered a terrible loss. It wasn't the right time to talk that kind of business with him."

"You're right," Kate said, sounding apologetic. "I had no idea that you were so close to them; really I didn't even know that you knew them personally. What are they like?"

Reina shrugged as if Kate could see her. "They're just regular people," she uttered. "Look, I just got home and I'm really tired, so I'll give you a call tomorrow."

"Okay," she responded reluctantly, clearly wanting to continue the conversation. "I'm glad you're back."

"Thank you," she said and then hung up without a goodbye. Reina leaned back in the recliner and tried to relax. It looked like this part of her plan was working out, but she didn't know for sure. She didn't want to consider what would happen if Traynor refused the job. It would certainly thwart her plans and she couldn't let that happen. He had to accept the job. It was best for everyone.

****

"Lord, I want vengeance," Traynor whispered. "I want Natalia to pay for what she did to my wife." Jessie Belle wasn't perfect, he knew that. In fact, she had done some terrible things. The memory of the day he found out that she had hired prostitutes for the convention in Miami rushed to the forefront of his mind. He remembered the night when he overheard his friends discussing her.

"I hear that it's Deveraux's wife that's in charge— she's the one those gals are working for. I heard it from the horse's mouth."

"No kidding? She's a madam?" asked the one named Sampson Taylor. "Man, are you sure about this?"

"If Jessie Belle's got herself a stable of girls working for her—that's for sho' what she is. That gal gon' bust hell wide open. Mark my words."

At the time, Traynor did not believe a word that he'd overheard. It was too crazy to believe that Jessie Belle would do something like that. However, when he found out the truth, Traynor had never felt such pain and disappointment in a person. He actually considered ending his marriage.

But marriage was a sacred commitment, and one that he took seriously. He had not only made a vow to Jessie

Belle—he had also made a vow to God. The crime she committed was serious, but Traynor had to discern if it was enough to file for divorce. He loved her and after some time passed and with God's help, he was able to forgive Jessie Belle.

He pushed that memory aside. Traynor did not want to remember his wife this way. He wanted to recall the way her eyes sparkled when she laughed, the way her smile lit up a room. Just the thought of her smile brought a smile to his face. In his mind, he could visualize the little pout she would make whenever she was trying to get him to see things her way.

Their marriage had been great once all the secrets were no longer between them. Jessie Belle turned her life around and he was proud of her. He loved her even more for how she had changed.

Traynor released a sigh of resignation as he pulled the covers down on the bed and climbed inside. Since Jessie Belle had passed away, he welcomed night more than he did each day. Because the darkness of the night matched the black hole in his soul.

And he didn't have any idea if that hole would ever again be filled.

****

"Even though I detested Jessie Belle, I kinda feel real bad for her son," Chrissy stated as she leaned back on the sofa and tucked her legs beneath her. She couldn't stop thinking about Jessie Belle, her death and her funeral. "I could see the grief all over his face. It was really heartbreaking."

"I know." Sabrina nodded. "I believe they were very close. She used to talk about him all the time."

"I don't think I've ever felt that way about anyone," she said, then she stopped. Chrissy wanted to talk about things she'd never shared before. But she wasn't sure how far she wanted to venture into her past with Sabrina. After a moment, she said, "I have no family ties to speak of."

"I know; you said you were abandoned by your parents, right?" Sabrina said without a hint of judgment in her tone.

Chrissy nodded. "I was told that my mother was a teenager and she just left me with some woman named Gloria Rick or Richards...something like that. I often wonder if my mother knew the woman she'd left me with."

"Maybe she was a relative, Chris," Sabrina said softly. "I don't think your mother would've left her child with a complete stranger. You'd have to be completely heartless to do something like that."

Chrissy shrugged. "I guess with most adoptions, the baby is left with strangers." She sighed. "Actually I hope that that woman wasn't a relative," she responded, trying to keep the emotion out of her voice. "Because I found out that she took me to a hospital and left me there. So I was abandoned twice."

"Oh, I didn't know that," Sabrina said.

"I know you didn't. I've never shared that with anyone."

"I'm so sorry," Sabrina murmured.

Chrissy swallowed hard, lifted her chin, and met her gaze. "It doesn't matter anymore. I eventually found my mother...."

Sabrina gasped.

"And ... she's dead now."

"Oh, no. Did you get a chance to at least talk to her before she died?"

Chrissy nodded. "It wasn't heartwarming or welcoming. She kept denying that she'd had a child when she was that young. So in a way, she kept denying me."

Sabrina was thoughtful for a moment. "Maybe she wasn't really denying you, Chris. I mean, how did you know it was really her? Maybe she wasn't really your mom."

"No. It was her. She was my mother. I took some hair from a hairbrush and had a DNA test done," Chrissy told her.

"Oh! So you knew her?"

"Not really. We weren't friends or anything. But when we met, I suspected it almost immediately."

"Why?" Sabrina asked.

Chrissy shook her head. She'd said enough. "All that matters to me now is that I know who my mother is—no idea about my father though, except that he might have been white."

Sabrina embraced her. "Well, you have me and I will always be here for you."

Chrissy hugged her friend back. "I'm grateful to have you in my life, Sabrina. I want you to know that. I really did miss you while I was gone."

When they broke apart, Sabrina said, "I really want you to consider giving up the life. We're getting older and the world's getting crazier by the minute."

Chrissy nodded. "I don't know what I'd do. The life is all I've ever known."

"Well, you have time to think about it and make some decisions," Sabrina stated. "I have three bedrooms, so you can stay here with me as long as you want."

That offer brought tears to Chrissy's eyes. "Thanks, girl."

"And I'd like for you to go to church with me on Sunday. I think you'd really like the pastor."

"Why?" Chrissy inquired, hoping that going to church wasn't going to be a requisite for her staying with Sabrina. "He has a heart for prostitutes?"

"Yes, but not in the way that you're thinking, Chris. He used to be one. You have to hear his testimony."

"Somebody from the life is now a pastor?" she exclaimed, then chuckled. "Girl, he just found another hustle. He ain't no real preacher."

Sabrina gave Chrissy a patient smile. "I know you don't have much faith in people. But there really are some good people in the world. There are really some people who try to do the right thing."

"They are few and far between."

"I hate seeing you so disillusioned, Chris," she said, shaking her head. "This is not the way to live."

"Maybe not for you." Her misery was so acute that it was a physical pain.

"I have hope."

She shuddered inwardly at the thought. "Sabrina, I'm happy for you, but we see the world differently. Always have. Always will."

"Will you at least think about coming with me, at least once? If it's not for you, that's fine. You never have to go back."

"I'll think about it," Chrissy responded, though she couldn't ever see herself going to church. She had no use for that place, but if agreeing to think about it made Sabrina feel good, then fine.

She told her friend what she needed to hear.

Chapter 8

Reina could not have been more thrilled when she heard that Traynor Deveraux had accepted the position as pastor of Bright Hope Christian Church. She had been the one who nominated him in the first place. ShHer hope had been that Jessie Belle would be coming with him, but her death changed all that.

Outside of Jessie Belle's passing, everything else was going the way she had planned it. She stared out of the huge window in her apartment and smiled to herself. Traynor belonged in a city like Raleigh, preaching to the wounded and lost souls. He was slowly dying in that small town and Reina wanted to spare him that. He deserved so much better.

He was such a good man, and she was so fascinated with him, that she was sure many would think that she had sexual motives. But her interest was purely platonic. Reina was not attracted to Traynor; she viewed him as a father figure instead.

The loud knock on her door made her turn away from the window and take quick strides across the room.

"I'm sorry it took so long," Kate said as she brushed past Reina. "Traffic was backed up on 540."

She really was not in the mood for company, but when Kate called and offered to pick up some dinner for them, Reina agreed to the visit. "You're fine."

Following her into the kitchen, Kate said, "I can't believe it. Pastor Deveraux is actually going to be our new pastor."

"I know," Reina responded with a smile. She retrieved two plates from the cabinet. "The shrimp scampi smells delicious."

"We have some fettuccine Alfredo, too. I asked for mushrooms to be added."

"You know me too well."

She nodded, then, "What do you think happened with Pastor Mike?" Kate asked as she fixed her plate. "I'm still in shock over his disappearance."

"Maybe he was burned out," Reina suggested, "and just needed a sabbatical."

"But if that were the case, then why did he stand in the pulpit and resign like that? What about Charlotte and Leah. Leah's only eight years old. Do you know the impact this is going to have on her?"

"Kate, I don't have any idea why he did what he did," Reina stated. "If I were to say anything, all I'd be doing is speculating. Maybe we should just wait and see what happens. Maybe he'll come back."

With their plates filled, they sat down at the breakfast table. Kate said the blessing before they sampled their pasta.

"You know, I'm actually surprised that you don't know more about what happened with Pastor Mike," Kate said in between a forkful. "I thought the two of you were pretty close."

Reina looked up from her plate, meeting her friend's gaze. "I don't know what gave you that idea. We were friendly, but that's about it."

Kate shook her head. "It seemed more than friendly to me. Maybe not on your end, but I think Pastor Mike was definitely attracted to you. I caught him plenty of times watching you, Reina."

"Don't be silly," she uttered. "You know, you shouldn't be saying stuff like this because we don't want rumors getting started."

"I was just saying …"

Reina cut her off. "I know what you're trying to imply, Kate, but you're wrong."

Her friend chewed on her bottom lip. "I didn't say you felt the same way about him."

"Can we just change the subject?" Her annoyance came through her tone.

"Sure."

After a moment, Reina said, "I'm sorry for snapping at you like that. I've just got a lot on my mind."

"It's okay."

She silently chided herself for the way she reacted to

Kate's comment. It was stupid. She definitely had to be more careful. There was no need to send out any warning signals to anyone.

As they ate, Reina tried to be more upbeat, and soon, Kate returned to normal. She filled Reina in on all she'd missed at church while she was away. Reina sat and listened as politely as she could. She hated gossip, but Kate loved it.

Then, Kate looked at her watch and announced, "I didn't realize it was this late. I need to get going." She scooped the last of her noodles off the plate. "I have to take my daughter to dance class."

"Just leave your plate there, I'll clean it up."

"Are you sure?"

"Yes," Reina said as she happily escorted her to the door.

As soon as Kate left, she cleaned up the kitchen, then rushed to her computer. Turning on her browser, she searched for the newspapers in Jacksonville, Florida and after a couple of minutes, paused when she saw a headline about a man who'd been found dead in his apartment. The property owner found him after neighbors complained of a foul odor. The authorities were still searching for the man's family because the name on the apartment rental lease hadn't led them to anyone.

Reina clicked off the computer, then picked up her family photo album. She had been doing a lot of that lately; thinking on the past. Normally, Reina did not like to dwell on those bad memories, but it was important for her to remember. Her recollection of all that had happened in her life is what fueled her.

So these memories were important. Especially now.

Chapter 9

"This is a pleasant surprise," Traynor murmured when Reina approached him after services ended. He had just finished his first sermon as the new pastor of Bright Hope.

He seemed surprised, but pleased to see her. "Are you a member of Bright Hope?"

Reina smiled and nodded. "I am. I'm so glad you accepted the offer to become our pastor."

He frowned, just a little. "Did you know about this when you were in Georgia?"

"I did," she confessed. "I didn't mention it because it just wasn't the right time.

I'd really hoped that your lovely wife would have been here with you."

He nodded as if he now understood. "In all honesty, I'm not sure I would've taken the job if Jessie Belle were still alive."

Reina made note of his comment in her head. As

much as she'd wanted Jessie Belle here too, maybe things had worked out the way they were supposed to. "How does it feel being back in Raleigh?" Reina asked.

He gave her a half-smile. "Bittersweet. I don't know if you know this, but Raleigh is where Jessie Belle and I spent most of our marriage. We have so many wonderful memories here."

Of course she knew that. Her tone was sincere when she said, "I pray it gets easier for you, Pastor, as time progresses."

"That's my prayer as well."

"I truly enjoyed your sermon on when God can't be explained. The truth is that tragedy is very hard to understand, hard to explain, and especially hard on faith."

He nodded. "Some people lay the blame at the feet of God and become bitter and cynical toward Him," Traynor said. "They ask for explanations, but get silence. They ask for understanding, and are baffled. My message this morning was for me as well."

"Life is a mystery, Pastor. Much of what happens is beyond us."

Traynor nodded in response. "Even if it were explained to us, we probably wouldn't be satisfied with the explanation. We just need to understand one fundamental truth that is spoken throughout the scriptures—the righteous live by faith."

Reina noticed that several people were behind her in the line, waiting to speak with Traynor. "I won't keep you any longer, Pastor. I'm glad you joined us at Bright

Hope."

The sensation that someone was watching her assailed Reina. Her eyes searched until her gaze met with the angry glare of the former first lady. She smiled and waved, but Charlotte Jennings turned her head away.

Her actions did not surprise Reina. Charlotte was cold to her even before she left for Florida. She was a jealous and suspicious wife who accused every good-looking woman in the church of having an affair with her husband.

Reina chuckled and quickly made her way out of the sanctuary before Kate could catch up with her. She was not in the mood today for the woman's constant stream of chattering. She felt good and wanted to keep it that way.

Her life was about to change and she couldn't be happier.

****

"I find it interesting that she just happened to be in Georgia for mom's funeral," Frankie said in a low voice, watching Reina's quick exit after she had held up the line speaking to Traynor. "And now she's here at this church. This is just too much of a coincidence, don't you think?"

Holt agreed. "I wonder if she knew about this when she came to Mom's service."

"She did," Traynor responded as he joined them near the pulpit, "but she knew it wasn't the right time to mention it to me, which I greatly appreciate." He paused. "Miss Cannon seems to be a nice person."

"She might be, but the question is why is she so interested in our family?" Holt stated. "It's not like she and Mom were really friends."

Traynor shrugged. "I guess I don't see it the way you and Frankie do. She doesn't seem to be any more interested in us than anyone else. I really don't think we have anything to worry about from that young woman."

Frankie gave a quick glance over her shoulder to make sure that Reina was gone before saying, "Pop, I don't know if you noticed, but she does seem pretty fond of you."

"She's just being nice," Traynor responded with a chuckle. "I'm old enough to be her father."

"Maybe she's looking for a father figure," Holt suggested.

"Or a sugar daddy," Frankie interjected, rubbing the roundness of her belly.

Traynor smiled. "Then she's certainly got the wrong man. I'm not interested in being anybody's sugar anything. I have no interest in ever marrying again. Your mother was my one and only soul mate."

Later that evening, Traynor laid in bed with the Bible opened beside him. He thought about what he'd told Holt and Frankie about Jessie Belle being his soul mate. That was true. That's why this hurt so much and that's why he had to fix it. The only way he could get rid of some of his pain was to make sure that Natalia paid for what she'd done.

First thing tomorrow morning, he was going to see Natalia at the law firm where she worked. Once he had evidence, Traynor intended to ruin her life just as she had ruined his.

****

Natalia walked out of her office in complete astonishment. "I was quite surprised when my assistant told me that you were here to see me," she said, looking at Traynor as he stood stiffly in front of her. "Why don't we go into my office?" She was glad to have this moment to talk to Traynor. Natalia didn't like the way they left things when she was in Georgia.

As she led the way, she attempted to make conversation. "I thought that we'd said everything when we were in Georgia, but I'm glad you stopped by. I didn't go there with the intention to upset you, Pastor Deveraux."

Traynor's lips thinned with anger, but he waited until they were inside her office before he said, "I only came here to tell you that I've moved back to Raleigh and I'm going to make sure that you pay for what you did to my wife."

Natalia closed the door behind him before stating, "And I told you that I had nothing to do with what happened to Jessie Belle. If I were guilty, why in the world would I have gone to the funeral? That's the last place I'd be."

"Perhaps you're feeling as if you're untouchable," he said. "You think you've gotten away with what you did, but you haven't. I'm asking the police to reopen the case."

Now, Natalia was pissed. "I'm an attorney. Police don't scare me." Her caramel brown eyes clawed him like talons. "I'm really trying to be sympathetic, but I'm tired of your accusations." Arms folded across her chest, Natalia continued, "If that is all you came to say, then I think it's best that you leave now before I have security throw you out, Pastor Deveraux."

"I'll leave, but just know that this isn't over. I am making it my business to see that you get everything you deserve." He glowered at her and then turned away, stomping out of her office.

For long after he left, Natalia couldn't sit down. His visit had shaken her to the core. She paced back and forth in her office. What was Traynor going to do? He could certainly make trouble for her. Especially if he really did know about her last conversation with Jessie Belle.

"Natalia …what are you doing here?"

"I came to see you, Jessie Belle," she replied, her tone cold and exact. "I remember how you came to visit me as soon as you heard my father was dead, however insincere it was. Well, I thought I'd repay the favor now that you're in that wheelchair."

"But how—"

Natalia cut her off. "I ran into Holt and his wife—

what he sees in that cow, I have no idea…. Anyway, I told him just how concerned I was about you and how much I missed talking to you. Holt gave me your address."

Natalia sat down in a nearby chair across from Jessie Belle. "So how's life treating you these days? Getting around much?"

"Excuse me?"

Natalia broke into a little laugh. "Oops, I'm sorry. That was pretty cruel of me, wasn't it?"

"Have you been drinking?" Jessie Belle asked.

"Of course not," she responded. "I don't drink, Jessie Belle. You know that."

"What are you doing here? I tried to call you before the accident. I wanted to talk to you. I—"

Natalia interrupted her by saying, "You know, I'm truly surprised you survived that nasty fall. I expected you to die. I guess you really are blessed and highly favored— that is what you're so fond of saying, isn't it?"

Jessie Belle did not respond.

"I keep going back to how you were so sweet to me after my daddy died. Back then, I thought to myself that you must really care about me."

"I do care about you, Natalia."

"Really? Is that why you forced my daddy to agree to the merger? Is that why you forced him—no, blackmailed him into stepping down as pastor?" She didn't give Jessie Belle a chance to respond. "Before he killed himself, my father wrote me a letter. I didn't know about the letter for a while, but once I found it and read it, I decided to make you pay."

Jessie Belle's eyes got wide. "It was you," she sputtered.

Natalia smiled. "You were always a smart woman." Opening her purse, she pulled out a knife.

"Oh, my God! Please don't kill me…," Jessie Belle pleaded, her voice trembling. She rolled her wheelchair back, but there was really nowhere to escape. "I'm begging you…."

"Why should I let you live?" Natalia spewed with hate in her tone. "Did my father plead with you to keep his secret? Did he beg you not to destroy my impression of him? Did he?"

There were tears in her eyes. "I was wrong for the way that I treated you and your family," Jessie Belle confessed. "But I'm not the same person I used to be— I've changed. Being like this… in this wheelchair… Natalia, I'm so sorry for the pain I caused you."

Natalia's eyes narrowed. "You'd say just about anything with a knife pointed at you—I'm not stupid."

"I'm paying for my sins. I'm paralyzed because of the mistakes I made."

It gave Natalia pleasure to watch Jessie Belle tremble in fear. For once, she was the one in charge. "Mistakes. Humph. You intentionally ruined lives. My father committed suicide because of you. My family name is ruined." She waved the knife in the air. "You haven't paid near enough for the pain you inflicted on others."

"I know that," Jessie Belle said. "Natalia, you can't know just how sorry I am."

Tears rolled down Jessie Belle's face, but Natalia did not feel an ounce of sympathy. "You deserve to be in that wheelchair and more," she hissed.

It was true that she had tormented Jessie Belle that day, but it was not as if the witch did not deserve what happened to her—she deserved that and more. However, if Traynor went to the police with his accusations, she could go to prison. Not for what she'd done, but for what Traynor was accusing her of doing.

Natalia had no alibi for the night that Jessie Belle had been pushed over the balcony. And she certainly had motive. Besides, she'd practically confessed to Jessie Belle; had Jessie Belle told Traynor?.

Natalia had to find a way to convince Traynor to keep his mouth shut. She was not going to prison for something she did not do.

Finally, she sat down at her desk, her mind spinning with thoughts. Then, she came up with a plan. If Traynor was determined to go the police, she'd just have to be ready. The only way she'd be able to save herself and clear her name was to find the real perpetrator.

But where would she start? Jessie Belle had made several enemies right here in Raleigh. Maybe it was one of her prostitutes. At least that was someplace to start.

She picked up her phone and dialed. As soon as Sabrina answered, Natalia said, "Can you meet me for lunch this afternoon?"

"Why?"

She was not surprised at her cousin's animosity. It wasn't like they talked often – really they didn't talk at all. She had hardly acknowledged her at Jessie Belle's funeral.

Still, they were family. And Natalia was annoyed that Sabrina would even question her. "Obviously, there's something I want to discuss with you," Natalia replied sharply.

"You don't need to take that tone with me," Sabrina stated. "You're the one who wants to see me, remember?"

"Sorry," she uttered as she massaged her forehead with her fingertips. "I'm having a stressful day."

After a slight pause, Sabrina said, "When do you want to meet and where?"

"How about one o'clock at Panera Bread on Capital?" Natalia suggested. "I'm going to be near there this afternoon."

"I'll see you then," she said and then hung up.

That had been a difficult call to make, especially since they weren't close. But with her plan, Natalia needed someone to talk to—someone she could trust. And no matter how she'd treated Sabrina, her cousin had never turned on her. Natalia knew that she could trust her and she hoped that Sabrina could shed some light on the other women who worked for Jessie Belle.

Two hours later, Natalia was saying, "Thanks for meeting me, cousin," when they slid into one of the booths at the restaurant.

"To be honest, I'm surprised you called," Sabrina said. "Especially since I never hear from you and then there was the way you snubbed me at Jessie Belle's funeral."

"I thought it was best that the Deverauxs had no idea of our connection,

Sabrina. Besides, I didn't expect to see you there and you had the nerve to attend with that so-called friend of yours."

"I don't know what's up with you and Chrissy, but I'm staying out of it. Anyway, what's going on?"

"One of the reasons I wanted to see you is to let you know that Traynor Deveraux is back in Raleigh," Natalia announced. "He came to see me this afternoon."

Sabrina's eyes widened in her surprise. "Why did he move back here?"

"Partly because of his son and grandchild, I imagine," Natalia stated.

Sabrina nodded. "Well, that makes sense."

"And, he's the new pastor of Bright Hope."

"Wow, I didn't know that."

Natalia continued, "But mostly I think he came here because he's also on a quest to find out who tried to kill Jessie Belle."

"Really? Why now? Why after all these years?" Sabrina questioned. "And why now, after she's gone."

Natalia gave a slight shrug. "He loved her and I guess he's on this mission out of some misguided loyalty to her."

Sabrina shrugged. "Well okay, but what does this have to do with me? Or you? Why did you want to see me?" Sabrina wanted to know. But then, she didn't give her cousin time to answer. "Wait. Do you think I had something to do with this?"

"Did you?" Natalia asked.

"No," Sabrina answered quickly. "I really liked Jessie Belle. She was good to all of the girls and she paid us well."

Natalia twisted her lips like she didn't believe her. "I'm pretty sure not all of the girls felt the same way about her as you do."

Sabrina thought for a moment. "Well, except for Chrissy. She hated Jessie Belle on sight. She called her a hypocrite, being that she was a pastor's wife. But I don't really think that was the real reason why she didn't like her."

"What do you think it was?"

"Chrissy had a bad experience working for a pimp, so she never liked working for other people. She preferred to strike out on her own."

"Well, I agree that Jessie Belle was a hypocrite," Natalia stated. "She held herself up as this pillar of Christianity and yet she had a stable of prostitutes; she was a blackmailer and who knows what else she's done."

"She was human," Sabrina defended her. "And really, Jessie Belle only supplied a need. I blame the men—the supposedly men of God who paid for our services. They were the real hypocrites. These were men who should have carried themselves beyond reproach. But they stood up in the pulpit and preached and then lived their private lives in sin."

"Good or bad, they are human as well," Natalia replied. "Look at my father; he loved the Lord. He truly did, but he had a sickness and Jessie Belle blackmailed him. It wasn't my father's fault. You can't blame him when one of his uncles molested him as a child. He never got over that."

Sabrina said nothing at first, though the look on her face said everything. With pity in her eyes, she finally said, "I loved Uncle John, but he was gay, Natalia." She kept her voice soft and without judgment. "He enjoyed having sex with men, pure and simple." When Natalia didn't protest, Sabrina continued, "My dad and your dad were brothers. And I know for a fact that there was no molestation. If there had been, my father would've known."

"Not necessarily!" Natalia exclaimed.

At first Sabrina shook her head, but then, she nodded at Natalia. "My father told me that your dad had always been attracted to men. From the time they were teens."

Natalia glared at Sabrina. "That's not true; he had a sickness, but he had it under control. My father was doing great, even after my mother died. And then, things changed when Jessie Belle Deveraux walked into our lives. She wanted my father's church—the church he labored to build."

"She did all of that to your father, yet you were willing

to marry her son."

"I loved Holt," Natalia said. "I wanted to be with Holt from the moment we met. My father's ministry was to merge with Traynor's after our wedding, but it was just a ploy on Jessie Belle's part." Natalia omitted her part in the plot. She didn't tell her cousin that she was the one who came up with the idea of the ministries merging because she desperately wanted to marry Holt and she knew that Jessie Belle would agree to that. Natalia continued, "Jessie Belle used all of us."

"Sounds like you really hated her, Natalia."

"I won't lie about it," she responded smoothly. "I do hate her. My father would still be here with me if it hadn't been for Jessie Belle. But I didn't push her."

"What do you mean? Why are you saying that?" Then, Sabrina's eyes got big.

Natalia nodded, knowing that now her cousin understood. She filled her in. "Traynor is accusing me of pushing her off the balcony. But even though I hated her, I would never do anything like that."

"But from all that you've told me, if Pastor Deveraux knows half of this, if he knows this is how you feel, then I have to say that he has a good reason for suspecting you."

She shook her head. "The way I see it—death was much too good for that woman. She would've suffered more by staying alive and not being able to do anything with those lifeless limbs, but sit and watch the world go by."

"Wow! That's harsh."

"That's how I feel."

"So, why did you want to see me?"

"I was just wondering...I was thinking about the women who worked for Jessie Belle. Maybe one of them did it."

Sabrina pressed her lips together before she said, "For the record, I didn't have anything to do with what happened to Jessie Belle and neither did Chrissy." Sabrina rose to her feet. "And another thing, from the way you're talking and if I didn't know you better, I would also assume that you were the one responsible for Jessie Belle's fall. You can't live with all of that hate in your heart, Natalia. She's gone, so let her rest in peace. You need to focus on your own life, cousin."

"I'm fine," Natalia huffed. "Instead of worrying about me—you need to work on your own salvation. You have a lot to be forgiven for, Sabrina."

Natalia's words stung, but Sabrina kept her expression blank. "I own everything I've done and I don't make excuses. Can you say the same?"

Natalia waved her hand in dismissal. "Bye."

Even after Sabrina turned and walked away, Natalia sat in the booth for a while longer, her mind swirling back to the day Jessie Belle found out that her father decided to turn down the merger. She had summoned Natalia to meet with her at the house.

"Why did you want to see me?" Natalie demanded to know upon her arrival.

"Your father's thinking of backing out of the

merger," Jessie Belle stated. "Did you know about this?"

"I hadn't heard anything." Natalia's eyes scanned her face. "How are you feeling since your heart attack?" she said, referring to the episode Jessie Belle had a few days after she found out that Holt had eloped with Frankie."

"I'm blessed to be alive."

"You're looking wonderful," Natalia complimented.

"I need you to talk to your father," Jessie Belle stated. "We need the merger to go as planned. Like you said when we came up with this idea, we need a larger church and your father needed more members. This hasn't changed."

She met Jessie Belle's gaze with a hard stare. "And what do I get in return?"

Jessie Belle sighed. "Natalia, my son is married now. There's nothing I can do about that."

"Then I'm afraid I can't help you, Mrs. Deveraux."

She glimpsed a flash of anger in Jessie Belle's eyes and noted the way she stiffened in her stance. "I held up my end of the bargain, Natalia."

Glancing down at her left hand, she responded, "I'm not the one with a wedding ring. The dark-skinned, plump girl with braids got the ring. The way I see it, when Holt rejected me—our deal was rendered null and void." Natalia turned and walked toward the door. "I'm glad to see you're doing so much better."

"You're making a mistake, Natalia," Jessie Belle warned. "If this merger does not happen, you and your father will regret this for the rest of your lives."

She paused for a moment before opening the door and turned around to face Jessie Belle. "This merger was my idea. I didn't get Holt and you won't get what you want. As you stated earlier, some things are beyond our control."

"This is far from over," Jessie Belle threatened.

"Bring it on," she said, issuing a challenge.

A few weeks later, her father was dead.

He died because of me, Natalia thought.

She felt the warm tears on her cheeks and she wiped them away. This was why it had been so important for her to make Jessie Belle pay. Jessie Belle had made good on her threat. Her father, the innocent victim in all of this, was dead. And she was glad that Jessie Belle had joined him.

But she wasn't going down for Jessie Belle's death. She would do whatever she had to do to protect herself.

****

Reina was in her office going over some documents when Kate rushed into her office, interrupting her. "What's going on?" Reina asked. "Why are you here?"

"You haven't heard?" Kate questioned. Her voice trembled.

"Heard what?"

"Pastor Jennings is dead," she announced. "They found him in an apartment in Jacksonville. The police say that it looks like he may have committed suicide. They found empty pill bottles."

"That's horrible, " Reina uttered without emotion, though she pressed her hand against her chest. "I was getting worried about him, but I never imagined that it would be this kind of news. It's awful."

Kate's eyes were bubbling up with tears. "What do you think made him do it? I know that he wasn't himself when he resigned, but to do something like this …I feel so bad for Charlotte and Leah."

"He committed suicide? Are you sure that's what the police said?"

She nodded. "Yes. They notified Charlotte this morning." Kate paused for a moment before saying, "I really feel bad for his little girl. How do you explain something like this to a child?"

"I'm sure Charlotte will wait until she's much older, but I'm not sure Leah will be able to handle it even then," Reina commented softly.

"This is just really crazy," Kate said as she fell into one of the chairs in front of Reina's desk.

She cleared her throat loudly. "I guess you never really know what people are going through."

Kate agreed. "I'm going over to see Charlotte. Do you want to come with me? It may do her some good to have friends around her."

"Why don't you go, Kate?" Reina suggested. "Charlotte may not want to be around a bunch of people right now. I know that I wouldn't, if I were in her shoes."

Kate studied Reina's words for a moment. "I hadn't

thought of that. I should probably stop and get a cake or pie…maybe some fried chicken."

"It most likely won't matter."

Reina sighed in relief when Kate stood and left without saying another word. As she stared at the door that her friend had just walked through, Reina said, "It's a good thing that I genuinely love her…she drives me nuts."

But then, her thoughts turned to the news that Kate had just shared with her. It had not taken as long as she initially thought for them to identify him, but Reina wasn't worried about it. He had stolen over fifty thousand dollars of church funds before he left town, hoping to start a new life with her. Following her instructions, he applied for the apartment under an assumed name, using a fake ID. So, it had been difficult for the police to track down his family.

Still, it had been a month, which had given her more than enough time to move on.

It was never Reina's plan to stay with him. She just needed him out of the way. And he was gone, for good now. And so Traynor would keep his rightful place at Bright Hope.

****

Traynor walked into his son's house and when he saw Holt and Frankie sitting in the living room, he told them the news. "I was informed today that Pastor Jennings was found in Florida. Apparently, it looks like he may have committed suicide. His wife called and asked me to conduct his home going service."

"That's horrible," Holt said, his eyes wide with shock. "Charlotte must be devastated."

"Where did they find him?" Frankie asked.

"He was living in an apartment in Jacksonville, Florida," Traynor replied. "He was registered under another name, so it took a while for them to find out his real identity."

"Charlotte told me that the night before he resigned, Pastor Mike told her that he wanted a divorce," Frankie said.

"Really?" Traynor and Holt responded in unison.

"She also told me that he took money from the church."

"There's money missing, though they've been trying to keep that under wraps," Traynor confirmed. "Maybe Mike was in some kind of trouble. Because none of this makes sense otherwise."

Holt agreed. "Frankie and I will go over tomorrow to talk with Charlotte."

"I would appreciate it," Traynor said. "I would go, too, but I don't know what to say right now. It was hard to talk to her on the phone. I guess this hits too close to home for me."

Holt nodded. "If you want, I can conduct the funeral service, Dad."

Traynor released a breath as if he were relieved. "I

may need you to do just that."

Later in his room, Traynor lay in bed with his eyes closed, though he couldn't sleep. In his mind, it was 1970 again.

He was in his new Ford Thunderbird that felt more like an oven as he drove to Mayville, Georgia.

He had no way of knowing this, but from the moment his father dispatched him to preach at Reverend Elias Holt's church for revival services, his fate was sealed. When Traynor parked his car in front of a little wooden house on Strawberry Lane, he had no idea what awaited him. He had no idea that he would find the love of his life in a dusty farming community. All he knew was that he was coming to preach the Word of God in a small town filled with people who loved the Lord. It was what he had been born to do—born to serve God with his entire being.

Traynor blinked back tears. He never doubted his calling until now. A range of emotions ran through him, pummeling him all over. No matter how he tried, he couldn't get over the pain of losing Jessie Belle. Traynor had conducted grief counseling for years, but taking his own advice was quite the challenge.

He wondered if he would ever be whole again.

Chapter 10

Mary Ellen was already at the restaurant by the time Frankie arrived. The two women embraced before being led to their table by the host. They decided to have lunch before engaging in some Christmas shopping.

"The last time I spoke to him, Traynor mentioned that he'd found a house already," Mary Ellen said once they were seated.

"He did," Frankie confirmed. "He's actually closing on it in a couple of days. I am so glad that he decided to move back to Raleigh. My husband really missed him."

"This change of pace will do him good," Mary Ellen stated.

Their server came to take their drink orders. She returned a few minutes later with two iced teas.

"Do you remember the woman that came to the funeral in the black widow garb?" Frankie asked.

Mary Ellen nodded. "I think that her name was Reina. Reina somebody. What about her?"

Frankie laid down her menu. "She's a member of

Bright Hope Christian Church."

Surprised, Mary Ellen asked, "Are you serious?"

Frankie nodded. "I find it a bit interesting that she shows up at the funeral and then Pop ends up pastoring at the very church where she is a member. Especially since she never once mentioned it when she came down to the service."

"Well, maybe she didn't think that was the appropriate time."

"That's what Pop said she told him, but still...."

"I agree with you, though; It is quite a coincidence," Mary Ellen acknowledged. "That's for sure."

"I have mixed feelings about her," Frankie confessed. "I'm not sure why, though.

She seems nice enough."

"I hear a but in your tone."

Frankie nodded. "But there's just something about her."

"Well, you know what to do. Just keep your eyes open and pray for discernment. God will reveal what you're supposed to know."

"You're right," Frankie murmured as she reached for her glass of iced tea. "I guess you heard about Pastor Jennings."

Mary Ellen nodded. "It's really sad, isn't it?"

"Yeah," Frankie murmured. "The man must have been really down about something to just resign and disappear like that...without a word to anyone. And now, Pop is leading that church." Frankie shook her head like it was all so unbelievable.

"I believe Jessie Belle would've been thrilled to come back to Raleigh." Mary Ellen took a sip of her tea. "In a way, I wish Traynor had been made this offer while she was still alive."

Frankie nodded. "We had a rough beginning, but I'm glad we were able to build a real fondness for one another."

"Jessie Belle and I were fast friends," Mary Ellen stated. "We hit it off from the very beginning."

The server returned to take their orders.

When she walked away, Mary Ellen continued, "She was definitely flawed, and at one point I was so angry with her, but when that attempt was made on Jessie Belle's life, I knew I couldn't stay mad with her. I had to forgive her."

"There are times when I wish we knew who hurt her, but then there's a part of me that is relieved that we don't really know. It's over now, but Pop is so angry. I can see it when he talks. He wants revenge, Mary Ellen. He wants revenge for what happened to Jessie Belle."

Mary Ellen sighed. "I feel so bad for him, but he's going to have to find a way to forgive. It's the only way he will truly find peace."

Their food arrived.

"He is so heartbroken," Frankie said. "Grief and anger…not a good combination. She was everything to him. And now, my hope is that Pop never finds the person who pushed Jessie Belle. He may be a pastor, but he is also human and I'm afraid of what he might do."

Mary Ellen waved her hand dismissing Frankie's concern. "Traynor loves the Lord and I know that God will be the one to help him through this." She smiled. "Besides, when those little girls get here—spoiling them will be the best thing for him. They will take his mind away from all of this."

Frankie nodded. "That's true. He and Junior are close," she stated. "He spends more time with Pop than he does his daddy, so Holt's feeling a little neglected." She chuckled.

"Use this time to spend some quality time with Holt."

Frankie laughed. "We're certainly doing that." Then her smile disappeared. "There are times when we feel guilty for being so happy. Holt is grieving, but at least we have each other."

Mary Ellen nodded in understanding. "Traynor is alone. I know how he may be feeling. I felt that way whenever I was around him and Jessie Belle after my divorce."

"He has us, but it's not the same."

"Frankie, don't worry. Traynor will be fine," Mary Ellen assured her.

Despite the assurance, Frankie's thoughts were dull and disquieting. She didn't know what it was, but she had a feeling that something bad was going to happen.

****

Chrissy sipped on white wine as she listened to the melodic sounds of jazz playing in the background. But the music could not quiet her thoughts as she paced in front of the substantial glass window that composed almost the entire wall of Sabrina's apartment.

What did I do to deserve this crappy life? I didn't ask to be born. My own mother didn't want me, so why didn't You just let me die? Did You put me on earth just to suffer? She didn't have to be a Christian to know that when God had it in for you—you were doomed.

She ran her hands through her hair, disheveling her curly locks, all the while trying to shake the negative thoughts from her mind. It wasn't good for her, according to her therapist.

She finished her glass of wine and then poured another.

She thought about her therapist – that was her secret shame. Something she hadn't even shared with her best friend. She began seeing a therapist after her diagnosis of bipolar disorder, but still, it was just one more thing to brand her as being worthless.

She had to find a way to look at the other side. Things were slowly turning around for her now that she was back in Raleigh. She had given up the life and gotten a real job as a receptionist for a realtor. She had even attended a few church services with Sabrina, although she did not attend consistently.

She was in her thirties now—life seemed to be passing her by. She wanted to stop the clock – actually what she really wanted was a do over, but there was no way it could happen.

Just like everybody else, Chrissy had to make do with the hand she was dealt in life. At least the one woman who could have destroyed her was dead, so her secrets were safe.

Sabrina joined her in the living room. "The music is nice, but sad," she told Chrissy.

"It suits my mood."

"Are you okay?"

She glanced over at Sabrina. "I'm fine." Chrissy knew that her friend was only trying to help, but she did not deserve help. She didn't want Sabrina to care. She knew that Sabrina wanted her to confide in her so that she could release the pain, but she wasn't ready to do that. Her soul was in agony, tormented by memories that she longed to forget.

She just didn't know what to do to stop her pain. She just didn't know how to forget.

****

Traynor had the movers take all of the boxes labeled 'Jessie Belle' up to the walk-in attic. He walked around his new home.

Jessie Belle would have preferred something much larger, but Traynor did not need a big house. The three bedrooms, office, family room and walk-in attic located on the third floor were enough for him. He chose it because he liked the size of the office and the master bedroom that was located on the first floor.

Traynor strolled over to the fireplace and sat a picture of Jessie Belle on the mantle. "I wish you were here with me," he whispered. His mind traveled back to a specific moment in time. When Traynor first realized that he could not live without her.

"You're so quiet," Jessie Belle said, cutting into his thoughts. "What are you thinking so hard about?"

"You," he confessed, turning so he could look into her eyes. "Jessie Belle, I've become quite fond of you. I … I don't want to leave."

Her gaze was as soft as a caress. "I feel the same way, Traynor."

He reached over, taking her by the hand. "The truth is…I've fallen in love with you. You're everything I've ever wanted in a woman. I know you're only eighteen, Jessie Belle, but you have such a warm spirit and you love the Lord—I can tell. I love that you don't mind being a woman and you're not out there trying to wear the pants."

She looked surprised by his admission. "Ooooh Traynor, I had no idea you felt this way about me. You've made me so happy." She paused a moment before saying, "But you live in Atlanta and I'm here in Mayville. I don't really see how a relationship will work out."

He nodded. "I've thought about that. I'm willing to drive down here to see you."

She frowned. "But with your responsibilities with the

church … Traynor, you just started pastoring there. That has to come first." Folding her hands in her lap, Jessie Belle added, "My parents won't let me come to visit you—they'd feel it was improper, you know. They're very strict. "

Her concern for his calling touched him. "I don't want to lose you, Jessie Belle."

"It's obvious that we both have deep feelings for each other. The challenge is gonna be in finding out how we can make this work."

Traynor had an overwhelming need to be close to her. It seemed like each day he spent with her—his feelings deepened and intensified.

Traynor silently considered his options. He was in love and there was only one thing to do. Kissing the back of her hand, he said, "I'll speak with your father later, but first, tell me about that little secret smile you have on your face? What does that mean?"

Her eyes met his. "I'm just happy, Traynor. Happier than I've ever been. I've never felt so in love. I think I can truly say that you're my first real love."

"It's the same for me."

After they finished eating, Jessie Belle took Traynor over to the stables to meet her horse, Diamond. "I've had her a long time—since she was a pony."

"I've never ridden a horse."

"Really?" she asked. "I love it. One day I'd like to own a couple of horses. I've always had this dream of me and my husband going riding in the mornings after breakfast and maybe in the evening right after dinner."

Happiness filled Traynor as he listened to Jessie Belle talk about her dreams. He wanted nothing more than to make them come true.

In the end, it was Jessie Belle's dreams that almost destroyed their marriage. If he had known how much power and control meant to her at that time, Traynor probably would have gone back to Atlanta without her.

But his undying love for Jessie Belle allowed her to get away with some of the awful things that she had done to others. Traynor never wanted to be a mega pastor or have a church congregation of thousands. That had been Jessie Belle's dream. The truth was that he had been his happiest pastoring at the small church in Mayville and living in Brookhaven. And he would have loved to stay there, but he couldn't. Not with the reminders of Jessie Belle everywhere.

Their souls were still connected. Traynor knew because he could not seem to let go of any of her things. For now, they would just sit up in the attic until he was ready to part from them.

****

The next day, Reina waited in the hallway for Traynor to leave his office. She had come to the church under the guise of dropping off the programs for the upcoming Christmas celebration.

She paced back and forth. Reina did not want it to

appear that she was waiting on him; she didn't want to be the subject of any church gossip.

When his door opened, Reina walked in the direction of his office.

Traynor stepped into the hallway. "Oh, Miss Cannon, how are you this evening?" he inquired.

She smiled. "I'm fine, Pastor. Have you gotten all settled into your new house?"

"I'm getting there."

"Just take it one day at a time," Reina advised. "You've been through a lot."

"Thank you for that, but it seems that I'm not the only one going through something. Everyone here has to be struggling through the same thing." When Reina frowned, Traynor said, "Your former pastor." "Oh, yes." Reina nodded. "It's very sad."

"Yes, it is," he agreed. "I met him some years ago and he was a very nice man."

"Pastor Mike was a good person," she stated. "It's really heartbreaking to learn just how troubled he must have been. I knew that he kept his emotions buried deep within—he was never one to complain."

Traynor frowned just a little. "You knew him that well?"

"Oh, no!" she said quickly. "I mean, I could just tell...that's what he probably did...." Her voice trailed off and inside she admonished herself. She really had to be careful with her words.

Traynor continued as if he accepted her explanation.

"I wish he had talked to somebody," he stated. "If only we could have had a conversation."

"I'm going to check on Charlotte tomorrow morning," Reina said. "This has to be really hard on her."

"I think she'll appreciate the company."

"I haven't experienced a loss like that, but I want to be there to support her." Then, she lifted up what she'd been holding in her hands. "This is a gift for you," she said, presenting him with the plant. "For your house."

He hesitated for a moment as if her gift surprised him. Then, he said, "Thank you, but I have to warn you, I'm not very good with plants. Jessie Belle was the one with the green thumb." Changing the subject, Traynor asked, "How long have you lived in Raleigh?" as he moved down the hall.

"For about five years now," Reina responded, following him.

"Where are you from originally?"

"I was born in Georgia, but raised in Florida."

His lips turned upward. "You know, I think my wife would have really liked you."

She smiled, but chose not to respond because she knew differently. Jessie Belle wanted nothing to do with her. But she would never tell Traynor that.

****

The casket holding the body of Pastor Michael Jennings had to remain closed during the funeral service since his body had deteriorated.

Reina sat near the back of the church so she could make a quick exit. Not only that, she didn't want Charlotte to see her. Charlotte had already demanded that a couple of the women she believed slept with Mike leave the services. The church was crowded, so by sitting in the back, it was not hard to stay out of her view.

She had not intended to come to the funeral, but Kate insisted that she needed to put in an appearance since she had worked on several committees under Pastor Mike's leadership.

As the services began, Reina frowned when she heard Charlotte sobbing loudly. There is no need for all of the drama, she thought.

She was sure Charlotte was upset, but would someone really be that grief-stricken over a man who abandoned her and his child? Not to mention bringing shame by stealing a bunch of money from a church. Reina did not want to be with anyone like that.

Charlotte's sobs grew louder.

I can't believe she's going to make Mike's funeral all about her.

She watched Charlotte's mother wrap an arm around Charlotte, trying to console her.

Reina released a soft sigh of relief when the choir stood up to sing and she felt even better when both Holt and Traynor stepped into the pulpit. Reina had heard that Holt would be the one to deliver the eulogy.

According to Kate, Charlotte initially put up a fuss,

wanting only Traynor to officiate her husband's services. But Frankie was able to calm her down before the situation escalated.

Mike had always told Reina that his wife was selfish, insecure, and jealous. Not to mention that she'd had a painkiller addiction in the past. These were the reasons he cited for cheating on Charlotte. Reina had never cared what his reasons were -- as long as her plan remained on track.

As she sat and listened to speaker after speaker, Reina had to admit there were some things she would miss about the man, but in the end, Reina was going to be fine, especially since this was all part of her plan.

When the service finally ended, Reina slipped out of the pew and headed straight toward the nearest exit. She heard someone call her name, but pretended otherwise. Reina quickened her pace, rushing out to her car.

Outside, Kate tried to flag her down, but Reina kept going. She'd paid her respects, there was no need to speak to anyone.

Her cell phone rang a few minutes later.

"Hello Kate," she said.

"Why did you leave in such a rush?"

"I need to get back to the shop," Reina responded. "It's a working day for me, you know."

"I was hoping you'd come with me to Charlotte's house. The poor thing was crying so hard. I just think we need to be there for her."

More like, Kate needs something to gossip about,

Reina thought. "Her parents and other relatives will be there, Kate. I don't think she needs us hanging around, too."

"That may be true." And then Kate went straight to what she did best. "Were you here when she made Joan and Amy leave?"

"Yeah, I saw that."

"I don't think Amy ever messed around with Pastor Mike," Kate said. "Joan…I wouldn't put it past her, though."

"I think it's all in Charlotte's head," Reina replied. "Mike is gone, so it really doesn't matter anymore."

"It matters to Charlotte."

She could care less, was what she wanted to say to Kate, but Reina remained silent.

"They're bringing the body out of the church. I have to go."

Reina pressed a button on the dashboard screen in her car to end the call. She had gotten out of there just in time.

Chapter 11

"Merry Christmas, Pop," Holt Jr. said when Frankie opened the door and Traynor stepped inside.

He pasted on a smile. "Merry Christmas." Traynor would have much preferred to spend this first major holiday without Jessie Belle in bed, but he knew it was the grief talking. Still, he didn't feel right about celebrating without his wife.

He hid his sadness behind a smile as he watched his grandson open his gifts. Traynor had brought Holt Jr. a bicycle and a set of toy cars and his grandson was thrilled.

"We have a white Christmas this year," Frankie said when she joined Traynor standing in front of the fireplace. "I've wanted one for years."

He stood, staring into the flames.

Holt walked over and stood on the other side of his father. "I miss her, too."

With his hand on the mantle, Traynor said, "Your mother loved Christmas."

"I know. She always went over the top with decorations, gifts…."

"Food," Traynor interjected with a short laugh.

Holt hesitated for a moment before he said, "Mom wouldn't want to see you like this, especially not on a day like today."

But it was as if Traynor didn't hear his son's words "If that night had never happened, son—your mother would probably be here with us right now. She would have been over there watching your child open his gifts."

"God doesn't make mistakes," he reminded his father. "None of this makes any sense to us, but we have to accept that mom leaving us when she did was a part of His plan."

"I'm angry," Traynor uttered aloud for the first time.

He didn't have any idea how his son would react, but Holt simply said, "God can bear your anger, Dad."

Frankie moved away, leaving the father with his son.

Traynor nodded, then said, "Right after your mother died, I considered walking away from the church."

"The way you stand up in the pulpit and preach—I couldn't tell. You still have the same passion and fire."

Another pause before Traynor said, "Each day, I ask God to decrease me and increase Him. I have to do that because my flesh craves the blood of the person who hurt your mother. Sometimes all I can think about is getting back at Natalia."

Holt looked at his father with curiosity. "Why do you believe that Natalia is that person, Dad? Have you really looked at her? She wouldn't have the strength to push anyone Mom's size with such force."

"I've thought about that," Traynor said. "But there are other ways. Natalia may not have been the one to push Jessie Belle, but that doesn't mean that she didn't hire someone to do the job."

"But who would she have hired. Remember, the police found no evidence of anyone breaking in."

"Exactly! I've always said that was a clue. That means that your mom knew her attacker," Traynor stated. When Holt shook his head, Traynor continued, "Son, I know you don't want to believe that Natalia is the one responsible, but she all but admitted it to Jessie Belle."

Holt took a quick breath. "I didn't know that. When was this?"

"She visited your mom after the accident. Natalia pulled a knife on her, threatened her and just about confessed."

He stared, complete surprise on his face. "Did you call the police? Why wasn't Natalia arrested?"

"Jessie Belle didn't want them involved. She felt she deserved what happened to her." Traynor glanced at his son. "Now that your mom's gone, I'm not going to let Natalia off. I intend to torment her like she tormented my wife."

Traynor saw the look of sorrow on his son's face, but there was nothing he could do about it. He was going to avenge his wife's death one way or another.

****

Reina found a spot on a pew near the front of the sanctuary at Bright Hope. There were quite a few members attending the Watch Night service to welcome in the New Year. Normally, she celebrated at a party, but this year, she decided to come out and support Traynor.

The moment she sat down she felt the heat of Frankie's gaze on her, and she resisted the urge to turn around. Now that Traynor was the pastor, Holt served as one of the assistant pastors, so Frankie was practically the First Lady. On the surface, Frankie was polite, but Reina was well aware that Frankie was studying her all the time.

A smile tugged at her lips. Soon, Frankie would see that she meant the family no harm. And soon, Frankie would be on her side.

Not too long after she took her seat, Traynor walked up to the podium. He seemed okay, but she knew him well enough now to glimpse the sadness in his gaze as he began his sermon.

"The door on last year has closed. The New Year has opened." Traynor's eyes traveled around the sanctuary. "It's a time to reflect back, and a time to look forward. To think of what is to come in this year. What we shall make of it, and what might it make of us."

Reina's heart swelled with pride as she listened to him.

"With the New Year, we start a new chapter of our life…."

She agreed. I've started a new chapter and this time it's all going to work out perfectly. This is the time of restoration for me—for all that I've lost.

"First, the psalm tells us that God is God, and we are not…It is God who brought the world, and us, you, me, into existence. It is God who brings life to an end …." His voice died suddenly. Traynor took a deep breath and exhaled slowly before continuing. "Time sets boundaries for us and it is out of our control. You and I are the same people we were as children. Time separates us from ourselves. We cannot live in yesterday; we cannot live in tomorrow, either. We are not only limited to the here, we are limited to the now. Don't waste your now worrying about yesterday or tomorrow."

Reina watched as Traynor ended his sermon and sat down. The pain of loss colored his expression. She wanted so much to help him through his grief, but she could do nothing. At least not yet.

Moments later, the clock struck midnight.

She sat in the pew as members of the congregation moved about murmuring greetings and well wishes to each other. Reina grabbed her Bible and designer handbag, preparing to leave. There was no one – except for Traynor and Holt – that she wanted to speak to.

Reina stood, stepped into the aisle, but before she could take another step, Charlotte suddenly appeared, blocking her path. "I'm surprised to see you here on New Year's Eve. You never came before. What's so special about this one?"

Her left hand clutched her designer purse so tight, Reina could feel her nails digging into her palm. Staring at the woman in front of her, she asked, "What exactly are you trying to imply?"

Charlotte glanced over her shoulder to where Traynor was standing, and then back at Reina. "You haven't a chance with him."

Reina let quiet stand between them for a moment before she said, "I wish you a very happy New Year."

"I don't want your well wishes, Reina," she growled. "Your words are hollow just like your heart." Charlotte paused a heartbeat before saying, "Oh and don't think, I didn't see you at Michael's funeral. I knew you didn't have enough class or manners to just stay away."

"Yeah, I was there for the show, but I have to tell you that your act needs a lot more work," Reina stated. "I'm sure you miss Mike, but you will enjoy the insurance money more." She ignored the way Charlotte glared at her. "C'mon, you were not happy when he upped and left you and Leah. He didn't love you anymore."

"You are such an evil woman," Charlotte spat. "I hope the Lord will strike you down and send you straight to hell where you belong."

Reina glanced around to see if anyone had heard Charlotte's words. When it didn't look as if anyone was paying attention to the two of them, she said, "You're not the first woman to wish me away and you probably won't be the last, but as you can see, I'm here and I'm not going anywhere."

"I knew that you were trouble from the moment I met you," Charlotte uttered.

Reina stepped closer to her and whispered, "When you look for trouble—you always find it."

Charlotte paused for a moment, and then she turned around and rushed away. Reina watched her until she disappeared into the sea of church members.

Her eyes traveled around the sanctuary searching for Frankie. When she could not find her, Reina heaved a sigh of relief. The last thing she wanted was for her to witness that exchange between her and Charlotte.

The church was serving a light meal, but Reina wouldn't be staying. Maybe if Charlotte had not come at her, she would have, but all she did at that moment was slip out one of the side doors and into the night.

****

"There's some tension between Reina and Charlotte," Frankie told Holt the next day as they sat down to breakfast together. "I saw them arguing after the service last night. I wonder what that could be about."

"Don't," Holt instructed.

"Don't what?"

"Don't get involved. Stay away from any church drama. Charlotte has already accused several women in the church of sleeping with Mike. And I don't know if that's true or not, but you know she's had some drug problems in the past."

"She may need a friend, Holt. Charlotte's angry, but she's hurting, too. Maybe I can get her into counseling."

He shook his head. "I don't know, babe."

"Let's invite her over for Junior's birthday party," Frankie said. "It'll give me a chance to get to know her better."

He eyed his wife. "Are you sure you want to take this on?"

"She's a member of Bright Hope, honey—the former first lady. We have to make ourselves available to her as we would any other member."

After a long moment, he agreed. "I know you can handle the women, but I don't want you to be overwhelmed right now. Maybe after the babies are born, then you can get involved. I know that they really need someone like you."

"If something is unsettled in a women's marriage or dating relationship, it's like nothing is right with the world until that is resolved, Holt. It really doesn't matter if it's a single woman or a woman married thirty years. We are relational creatures and it's hard for some women to thrive in life if they're not thriving in relationships. I can help these women."

He released a long breath.

She said, "I want to do this for all of us. For you an Pop, too. A church divided cannot stand and Charlotte's actions and accusations are causing problems between the women of the church."

"Okay, if you think that will help Charlotte."

"It will. And it will help the other women in the church." She paused. "Including Reina."

"What help does Reina need?"

"Well, she comes off as being very confident in who she is, unlike Charlotte.

However, I feel like Reina is searching for something—I don't know what it is, although I think part of her problem is that she has eyes for Pop. Have you noticed how she hangs on his every word?"

Holt laughed. "You really think she has a crush on him?"

She didn't laugh with her husband. "I'm not sure. I mean, for what other reason would she be trying so hard to connect with him?"

Holt continued chuckling, but Frankie didn't crack a smile. She didn't care what her husband said. She knew women. And she knew that Reina was a woman to be watched.

****

Traynor decided to have lunch at Fitzgerald's. He loved seafood and it was one of Jessie Belle's favorite restaurants. He'd planned on dining alone and he was fine with that. So when Reina walked up to his table, she caught him off guard. She removed her coat revealing the red dress underneath, the way her hair flowed in loose curls around her face…Traynor blinked. For a moment she reminded him of his wife. It was the first time he noticed the tiny mole on her lip.

"Pastor Deveraux, I thought it was you."

"H-Hello Reina. How are you doing?" Traynor struggled to recover from his staring. Reina did not look anything like his wife, but.... He shook off his confusion.

"I'm fine, but it's really cold out there."

He agreed, although his mind was not on the conversation.

"Are you eating alone?" she asked, cutting into his thoughts.

"Yes." Traynor did not know why he was reacting this way. It had to be grief, he surmised. It caused him to see Jessie Belle in everything and everyone and now even in Reina.

"Do you mind if I join you?"

He rose to his feet. "Excuse my rudeness."

She eyed him for a moment. "You look like you have something on your mind. Are you okay?"

Traynor smiled. "I'm fine."

"Are you sure I'm not intruding?" she asked although she was already halfway down in her seat.

"I don't like to eat alone," he said quietly. "I welcome your company."

As he returned to his seat, Traynor was tormented by confusing emotions.

"I hear your daughter-in-law will be taking over the women's ministry," Reina stated. "I hope she knows what she's getting into."

Traynor regained his composure. "Frankie will be

good for the women there."

"I stopped participating a while back, but now that we have new leadership in place—I may start up again."

He nodded. "I think you should."

The server took their orders.

When the waiter left them alone, Reina said, "Pastor Deveraux, it's okay if you want to talk about your wife. I'd like to hear about her. Like how did you two meet?"

He hesitated, not sure that he should be having this conversation with one of his church members. Especially not one he had just met. Especially not a women. But there was something about Reina. So, he said, "I preached at her father's church for a revival. We met, fell in love, and got married two weeks later. I suppose you can say that it was love at first sight."

"Wow," Reina said, grinning. "I love it. You and Jessie Belle knew what you wanted and you didn't waste any time."

"My heart knew hers."

She met his gaze. "That's beautiful."

Their food arrived and Traynor blessed their meals. After that, it was easy for him to tell her the rest of the story.

"After we got married, she and I moved to Atlanta," he said, picking the conversation right back up. "That's where we started our life together. That's where she met Mary Ellen—they became life-long friends."

"She runs the radio station, right?" Reina asked.

"Yes."

"After Atlanta, you and Jessie Belle moved to Raleigh or did you live somewhere else?"

"I was offered a job at New Salem Baptist."

"Really? I had no idea that you once pastored there. It's right down the street from my hair salon."

Traynor wiped his mouth with the edge of his napkin. "It was a long time ago."

"You have lots of wonderful memories."

"I do," he acknowledged. "We had a good life. Moving to Raleigh was the best decision we made." At least in the beginning, he added silently. Then things went downhill with Jessie Belle's lies and deceit. Traynor pushed those negative feelings away. He didn't want to remember the turbulent years, especially after all his wife had done to redeem herself.

All he wanted to remember was the love.

****

Reina walked into her house grinning.

She couldn't believe the look on Traynor's face when he had looked up to see her standing there. She had chosen her outfit deliberately. She had a picture of Jessie Belle wearing something similar, and she'd been curious as to how Traynor would respond when he saw her.

Reina knew he would be there because she had followed him from the church. She had been on her way to see him when she spotted him leaving. So, she just got into her car and then gave him a few minutes to get settled in the restaurant before she went in.

Her thoughts were still on him when she changed into a pair of yoga pants and a tank top and then she left the house to go to the gym. Inside her car, she remembered the way Traynor had looked at her when he glanced up and saw her.

At first, he looked as if he had seen a ghost and she felt bad about that. She was not trying to torment him; she just wanted to see his reaction.

After her aerobics class, she returned home, stumbling her sore body into the bathroom where she started the hot water for a shower. The steaming water pelted her back while she contemplated her next move since after today's lunch, she knew that she was getting close.

Reina dried off, wrapping a towel around her body before walking into the bedroom. She dressed in a pair of jeans and a sweatshirt. Her body was still sore from her workout, but she wasn't going to complain. She promised herself that she would go to the gym at least three days a week so that her body would be ready for the spring..

At thirty-two, she looked great. In February, she would turn a year older and she wanted to continue looking her best.

Reina touched her flat stomach and whenever she did that, her smile dimmed just a little. She'd accepted the fact that she would never be able to bear a child. But even though she'd come to terms with that, it was hard because there would be no one to carry out her legacy—

no family to love and cherish.

That was why her plan was so important. All of that would change very soon.

Chapter 12

Natalia looked forward to the annual charity event for the North Carolina Pediatric Association every year. She had worked on the planning committee and was thrilled that everyone agreed to the Mardi Gras theme. Now, as she navigated around the room, she did all of her last minute checks to make sure that everything was in the right place.

The room glistened with elaborate white marble columns and a dance floor made of slate. Massive floral arrangements and large elegant masks were placed sporadically throughout the room. The idea was to create a fun atmosphere where attendees could enjoy good music and great food while letting their hair down with outrageous costumes…and of course, the requisite bead necklaces.

As the ballroom began to fill up with guests, Natalia checked on the items that were up for auction, and she rearranged a few for premium placement. She smiled in satisfaction. "This looks much better."

Next on her mental checklist was to see how the wine tasting was going. But just as she was moving to the other side of the room, Natalia muttered a curse under her breath when she spotted Mary Ellen walking toward her.

"Don't look so worried, I'm not here to see you," Mary Ellen said, speaking above the music from the band that began to play on the stage..

Natalia eyed the black gown Mary Ellen wore and chuckled. That dress paled in comparison to her royal purple and gold ball gown. "I'm not worried about anything and especially not you."

Mary Ellen's eyes traveled the room. "Everything looks wonderful. See what happens when you use your powers for good."

She refused to let Mary Ellen get to her and decided this was a good time to tell Mary Ellen something that had been on her mind.. "I saw how attentive you were to Traynor during the funeral. I really hope you don't have your eyes on him." The shock on Mary Ellen's face almost made Natalia laugh. Instead she finished with, "I'm afraid you're not even close to the woman that Jessie Belle was."

Mary Ellen recovered quickly and broke into a grin. "Traynor and I are just friends, but I'm sure that it's much too taxing on your brain to understand something like friendship."

"You just remember that on those cold, lonely nights."

"Sweetie, my nights are anything but cold and lonely,"

Mary Ellen countered. "Don't worry about me, Natalia. Focus on your own life … oh that's right … you don't have one."

"Cute," she murmured in response. "Well, I see some people I really want to talk to, so I'll be on my way."

"Enjoy your evening," Mary Ellen said.

Natalia sent her a sharp glare before walking away. "I can't stand that woman," she muttered under her breath. But then with Mary Ellen there, Natalia had another thought. She hoped that Traynor would not be coming to the event—she didn't want him to ruin it for her.

She had not seen him since the day he showed up at her office and she hoped that maybe with the passage of time, Traynor had decided not to pursue his claims that she attacked Jessie Belle. She hadn't made any headway into finding out who had really attacked Jessie Belle. Not that she'd done any more investigating after talking to Sabrina. Her cousin hadn't been able to help her – it had been a dead end.

But her thoughts were interrupted, when she noticed a woman coming through the door. "Well…isn't this interesting," she murmured.

Just as she moved toward the door, she heard, "Would you like to dance?" from a deep baritone voice.

Turning around, she looked up at the handsome face that went with the voice. "Could you ask me again in about ten minutes, please? There's someone I really need to have a conversation with, but I promise I'll be back."

He smiled. "And, I'll be back in ten minutes."

"Okay," she responded with a grin.

Natalia hoped that the handsome man would keep his promise. Her evening was looking up. But first, there was something that she had to do.

****

"Are you stalking me?" Reina asked when Natalia sat down at her table without invitation.

"I was just about to ask you the same thing."

"I'm here to support the foundation." Reina took a sip of her champagne. "If I'm not mistaken, your table is somewhere in the back."

"You're wrong," Natalia quipped. "I'm right over there." She pointed to a table near the stage. "I'm on the board."

"Goody for you."

Natalia chuckled. "Is that all you have?"

"Honey, go find someone else to annoy," Reina uttered with a sigh. "I intend to enjoy my evening."

"I'll leave in just a moment, but first, I want to say something to you." She paused, though she wasn't asking for permission to proceed. "From what I've heard, you have been spending a lot of time with Traynor Deveraux."

Reina met her gaze. "And?"

"Well, his wife is barely cold in her grave. I would think you would be more discreet. Besides, I'm sure he would choose Mary Ellen before he'd even look at you."

"It must be so awful to not have a life of your own," Reina stated. "I feel sorry for you."

"Hummph," Natalia huffed, wondering why everyone thought she didn't have a life. "I don't need your pity. I have a full life." She thought of the handsome man that she promised a dance, prompting an unconscious smile to form. She glanced over her shoulder to where Mary Ellen stood talking to another guest. "I just have to say that you and your competition over there have nothing to offer Traynor Deveraux," Natalia said. "He's grieving and you both need to stay out of his face."

"I see misery still loves company," Reina stated. "He won't have anything to do with you, so you're jealous that we are a part of his inner circle."

Natalia burst into laughter. "You. A part of his inner circle. Girl, you have had way too many drinks tonight and the party just got started. You aren't even a part of Traynor's outer circle. He merely tolerates you."

Those words made Reina glare at her. "You have no idea what you're talking about."

"I've heard that you've been trying to force your way into his life," Natalia pushed, sensing that she'd gotten to Reina. "Really, it's so pathetic."

"I think you need to leave," Reina said, her lips barely moving.

Natalia pretended to be afraid. "Or what? What are you going to do to me?"

"What is it with you?" Reina asked. "You don't like me and I don't like you either. We're clear on this, so just stay away from me."

"You're right," Natalia confirmed. "I don't like you. But I really care about Traynor and Holt."

"I'm sure they are capable of taking care of themselves." Reina impaled her with her eyes.

Natalia pushed away from the table and stood up. "Just leave them alone. And while you're doing that, watch your back."

"Always," Reina responded, even though Natalia had already sashayed away.

****

Natalia's eyes searched the room for the handsome man in the black tuxedo to whom she had promised a dance.

She found him standing a few yards from her table and Natalia strolled toward him. Before she reached him, he looked up, and moved toward her, meeting her halfway.

"My name is Dean," he said, holding his arm out to her.

She hooked her arm through his. "Natalia," she said, as he swept her onto the dance floor.

They danced across the floor, to the first song and then another. Song after song. She hadn't had this much fun in a long time.

"I'm afraid I'm going to need to sit this one out," Natalia said after what felt like an hour-long dance marathon. "I haven't danced this much since college." She used her hand to fan herself.

He flashed her a sexy grin. "You're in great shape. I noticed that when I saw you a couple of weeks ago at the courthouse," Dean stated. "I've been trying to meet you ever since. I thought I was going to have to show up at the law firm where you work."

She stopped fanning herself. "Please don't tell me that you're a stalker."

He laughed. "I just realized just how creepy that sounded. No, I'm not stalking you, Natalia. I simply want to get to know you."

She pretended to give his words some thought, even though she knew he wasn't a stalker. She knew exactly who this man was – though, she kept that to herself. When he held his hand out to her, she took it and they hit the dance floor again.

She and Dean danced intermittently for the next three hours and it was hard because while she wanted to enjoy herself, Natalia had to remind herself that she was working the event.

During one of their breaks, Dean led her outside. "I hope I've eased your mind some," he said as they strolled outside on the terrace.

She smiled. "I suppose you're not a stalker. I wasn't going to tell you, but I've actually heard of you. You handled the Corden case last year."

He nodded and grinned as if he were happy that she recognized him. "I don't think I've ever worked so hard in my life for a client. Hector Cordon was innocent and I'm glad we were able to prove it."

"And right after that case, I found out that you were a pastor, too. That surprised me."

He nodded. "I've been an associate pastor for almost three years," Dean stated.

"My father was John Winters," she told him.

His eyes widened. "I had no idea," he responded. "He was someone I admired. He often lectured at the seminary I attended."

"He loved lecturing," Natalia said softly. "My father was offered a full-time position at the college, which he was considering until…"

He waited a moment before he said, "I'm sorry for your loss, Natalia. I heard he'd passed away a few years ago."

"Thank you," she murmured, turning away from him for a moment. "I miss both my parents a lot."

"I'm very close to mine, so I can't imagine what you have been going through."

Returning her gaze to him, she half-smiled. "Even though it's been three years, I'm still taking it day by day."

His dark eyes reflected glimmers of light. Natalia couldn't stop herself from staring into them.

After a moment, he said, "Let me get you back inside. I'm sure you must be cold."

"Just a little," Natalia admitted. But before she took a step, she added, "I've enjoyed talking to you, Dean." Something in his manner soothed her spirit.

It felt like he was caressing her with his eyes when he said, "I hope this won't be the last time I get to enjoy your company."

Smiling demurely, she asked, "Is that your way of asking me out on a date?"

They held each other's gaze and then, Dean grinned. "Is it working?"

"Let's have one more dance and I'll let you know," she murmured.

They laughed together as they strutted back into the ballroom.

****

Chrissy eyed her reflection in the mirror. Now that she was thirty-three, she had so many decisions to make.

She enjoyed working at the real estate office, but it was part-time and she needed to make more money. She'd been considering getting her license to sell real estate, but Chrissy had not quite made up her mind yet.

It felt like her life was opening up. With the help of her therapist and even church, Chrissy finally had hope for the future. Actually, she hadn't noticed it right away, but she'd found a measure of peace when she'd been told that her mother passed away. That's when this all started – her journey to a better life. She was discovering her life in the death of the woman who gave birth to her.

Chrissy glanced over at the Bible Sabrina had given her for Christmas. She reached for it, then blew away the light film of dust that covered it. Although she attended church more than before, Chrissy still had no interest in reading scriptures.

She heard Sabrina in the kitchen, probably getting ready to cook dinner for them. Chrissy did all of the cleaning while Sabrina prepared all of the meals since she was the one who was the wonderful cook.

Usually Chrissy would sit with Sabrina while she prepared their meals, but tonight, Chrissy wasn't in the mood for conversation, so she stayed inside her room. Sabrina would understand. They were the perfect roommates since Sabrina understood Chrissy's mood swings. And it helped that Sabrina never pushed Chrissy into attending church. When Chrissy did not want to go, Sabrina simply left her alone.

She sat up, propping herself against her pillows. Then, she opened the drawer to her nightstand, took out the pill bottle, and popped a pill into her mouth. It had been a struggle, but she kept her promise to her therapist – and to herself. She had stayed on her medication.

Opening the blinds that covered her window, she took in the scene outside.

The trees were bare, making the air look cold and dismal. Her favorite season was fall in Raleigh—when the trees were various shades of gold, red and brown. It was always just so beautiful…she was amazed at God's ability to create such beauty in the world, but then allow that beauty to be marred by the ugliness of horrific people.

Whenever she looked at the creation around her, she

had to question God. There were so many things that she didn't understand. Like how Pastor Poolee said that God hated sin. "So why do You allow these things to happen?" she whispered.

From the times when she attended church, Chrissy learned that God could compensate for people's evil actions through supernatural intervention. He could stop a drunk driver from causing an automobile accident. He could stop a man addicted to drugs from doing any harm to his wife, children, or extended family. "Why do You sit in judgment of sins when it is under Your control? Why not do something?"

When she asked Sabrina similar questions, her response was always the same, "Don't give up on God. Trust Him through the good and the bad."

Chrissy really wanted to do that, but even with the way her life was turning around, she couldn't. She wanted to turn to God and turn everything over to Him, but in her heart, she knew that there was no way that God could really accept her.

Sabrina had worked hard, trying to save Chrissy's soul. But what Chrissy just couldn't seem to get Sabrina to understand was that her soul was beyond saving. There would never be any redemption for her.

And as much as she hated to admit it, that made Chrissy sad. Very sad. Even though today was a special day.

****

"Happy Birthday to me," Reina said softly before taking a sip of champagne. Earlier in the day, her staff had gotten together to celebrate her birthday at a restaurant in North Hills. They gave her a two hundred dollar gift card, which she planned to spend on a new outfit. It was time to start building her spring wardrobe.

"You look fabulous for thirty-three," she told herself.

Reina strolled over to the full-length mirror in her salon and posed. She could have been a model when she was younger, but shied away after hearing all of the horror stories. There was no way she would let someone try to control her ever again. It was not in her DNA.

Her staff had gone home hours ago, but Reina stayed behind, enjoying the solitude. Plus, Reina didn't want to go home to an empty house. So, she sat in front of the mirror and sipped champagne until she decided to call a friend.

Keith. She had not spoken to him in a few months, but it didn't matter. Their relationship was strictly a physical one.

She finished off her champagne, picked up her purse, and turned on the alarm before leaving. Her Lexus was parked in front of the salon so she didn't have far to walk.

Twenty minutes later, she was ringing the doorbell to Keith's townhouse.

"Hey, beautiful," he greeted.

Reina smiled. "Hey, yourself."

He kissed her. "I missed you. Where have you been?"

"I was out of town for a while, but I'm back now," she responded. "Do you really want to spend all this time talking?" Reina unzipped her dress and let it fall in a puddle around her feet.

Grinning, Keith shook his head, his eyes pleading for her to continue.

She did a little striptease, removing each item in a slow, tantalizing way. When he could not bear to keep his hands off her, Keith picked her up, carrying her naked into the bedroom.

Two hours later, she lay in bed, her body intertwined with his. Reina tried to break free without disturbing him.

"Where you trying to go?" he mumbled sleepily.

"I need to go home," Reina responded. "Tonight was great, but it's time I get out of here."

"Why don't you spend the night? Sina won't be home until Thursday."

His live-in girlfriend was a flight attendant. Reina enjoyed spending time with Keith because he was not in a position to make demands on her time. He just fulfilled a need in her and she expected nothing more.

This way, there was no disappointment. She had had enough of that to last her a lifetime. So she kissed Keith, got dressed and went on her way.

She had gotten what she wanted out of that night.

Chapter 13

The church service had just ended when Reina heard a voice behind her.

"What are you up to?"

She turned around and faced Frankie. "I'm not sure I know what you mean," Reina responded smoothly.

"And I don't know. I can't quite put my finger on it, but it seems like you've taken quite an interest in my family." Frankie paused. "Why is that?"

Reina released a soft chuckle. "Look, I'm not after your husband if that's what you're thinking."

"What about my father-in-law?" Frankie wanted to know. "I heard you had lunch with him the other day."

"Oh," Reina said, and waved her hand. "I just happened to run into him."

"I don't believe you," Frankie said. "Are you after him?"

Reina shook her head and chuckled. "No, not at all. He is like a father to me. Nothing more, I assure you." It was the way that Frankie narrowed her eyes that made Reina continue, "I have no ulterior motives. I like you all and I assumed the feeling was mutual. Am I wrong?"

Frankie waited a moment before she said, "I just want to understand."

"Well, let me explain it to you. It's not like I don't have friends," Reina stated, "because I do. I am very selective who I associate with—I'm sure you've noticed that the women in this church have drama going on and I'm not looking to be a part of that."

"Well, what about your family? Do you have family in the area?"

She met Frankie's gaze straight on. "Why do you ask? What does that have to do with anything?"

"I would like to know more about you since you've made it your business to know more about us. And I figure it's always best to get my information first hand, don't you agree?"

"Yes," Reina stated. "So to answer your question— no, I don't have any family in the area. I don't have any family anywhere really. Unfortunately, everyone is dead as far as I know."

The ends of Frankie's lips turned down slightly. "I'm sorry to hear this."

Reina shrugged. "I used to wonder why I was born into the life I was given, but eventually I just accepted that I was not blessed with a large family."

"You do have family, Reina," Frankie responded, softening now. "They may not be blood relatives, but you are loved by your friends and church members. We are your extended family."

Reina sighed with relief. "I guess that's why I have been so drawn to your family. I love the closeness you all share. And I, for one can see how protective you are," she chuckled, "and I love that. If I had family, I'd be the very same way."

Frankie nodded.

Reina continued, "Holt Jr. is so adorable and loving—I feel like he's my nephew and I can't wait to meet your daughters," she said glancing at Frankie's swollen belly. "I love children and this will be as close as I get to having any."

Frankie smiled warmly. "You're right. I am very protective of Traynor, Holt and my children. And that's why I was so…curious about you."

"I understand. You and Jessie Belle must have been very close," Reina stated. "I imagine that she felt the same way."

"She did," Frankie said. "You knew her, right? My mother-in-law?"

Reina nodded.

Frankie asked, "How exactly did you know my mother-in-law? I know her hairstylist and she was with Dee for years."

"I met her at a conference," Reina responded. "I gave her my card and she came to see me once. I think she said that her stylist was on vacation or something, but she needed to get her hair done for some big event."

"You only saw her that one time?" Frankie asked. She had softened, but she was still clearly trying to put the pieces together.

"No, we ran into each other at several functions over the years." When Frankie's eyes narrowed once again, Reina added, " I never said that we were close friends, Frankie, but we were not strangers either. Jessie Belle didn't trust too many women."

"You're right about that." Frankie nodded.. "Mary Ellen was that one friend and confident—my mother-in-law was fine with one good friend."

"I hope that this eases your mind some," Reina said. "Because I'd like to host a baby shower for you here at the church."

"It does," Frankie replied. "But you don't have to go through the trouble of throwing me a shower."

"It's no trouble at all. We do this for all of our expectant members."

Frankie smiled. "Well, thank you. And you know what? I'm glad we were able to have this conversation."

"Me, too," Reina responded, a smile plastered on her face. The smile stayed there until Frankie turned away.

She hoped this would put an end to Frankie's suspicions. She preferred having her for a friend and not an enemy because it would not turn out well for either of them if she had to put Frankie into the enemy category..

****

Reina held up a dress in front of her as she stared at her reflection in a mirror. She'd decided to spend her lunch hour shopping at Crabtree Valley Mall and Macy's was one of her favorite stores so it was her first stop.

"Well, it seems as if I'm seeing you everywhere," Natalia said as she came up behind Reina. "Before Jessie Belle's funeral, I don't recall ever running into you."

Reina rolled her eyes.

That didn't stop Natalia from continuing. "I must have run into you though, because you seem very familiar to me."

Turning to face her, Reina said, "I assure you that we've never met before the funeral." She put on a smile as she returned the dress back to the rack. The last person she wanted to deal with right now was this little twit. Natalia had placed a damper on her mood.

Reina turned away from her, hoping she would take the hint and walk away.

No such luck.

Natalia strolled around to the other side of the clothing rack so that she stood facing Reina. "So tell me … did you have something to do with Traynor becoming pastor of Bright Hope? Is that why you were in Georgia? To persuade him to return to Raleigh?"

She laughed. "Natalia, I can't imagine why you're so interested in Pastor Deveraux's return to Raleigh. You're really straining your brain trying to figure out something that has nothing to do with you. All you need to know is that Traynor is out to get you."

Natalia frowned. "Did he tell you that?"

Reina noted that Natalia attempted to look confident, but her lip quivered. "It doesn't take a rocket scientist to figure out that he blames you for what happened to his wife," she said, recalling the conversation between Holt and Mary Ellen that she overheard at the repast.

"He's wrong about me," Natalia stated. "Jessie Belle is the one responsible for what happened to her."

Reina eyed her a moment before asking, "I'd like to know something. Why did you have a problem with Jessie Belle?"

"She was a horrible person," she simply stated..

She raised her brow at Natalia's response. "Why do you say that?"

"Trust me when I say that I have my reasons," Natalia uttered, switching her Coach purse from one shoulder to the other.

"Why does Traynor blame you?"

Natalia shook her head slightly. "I'm not going to discuss that with you."

Reina chuckled. "Well, here's some advice," she began, "stay away from Traynor unless you want to find yourself in a jail cell."

Natalia did not respond.

Reina turned and walked away, grinning. She had no idea if Traynor would go that far, but it was enough to shut Natalia up.

She left Macy's having lost her desire to shop and instead headed to Kate's house. Once she settled inside,

Reina asked Kate, "Do you know Natalia Winters?"

They sat in the family room, so that Kate could keep an eye on her daughter, who was working on a school project at the breakfast table.

"Yeah. Her father was the pastor of Mt. Vernon Baptist Church. Soon after Pastor Deveraux took over his church, he committed suicide."

"Really? She's John Winter's daughter?"

Kate nodded.

"So do you know Natalia personally?"

"We used to be close friends," Kate responded. "The last time I really talked to her was when she told me that she and Holt Deveraux were supposed to get married, but that never happened. And when he married someone else, Natalia was furious. She blamed his mother for keeping them apart."

"Interesting," Reina said, nodding at the news.

"I know." Kate continued, "After her father killed himself, she fell out with Jessie Belle for good."

Reina searched her memory. "I think I did hear about Pastor Winter's suicide and I knew that Traynor took over the church, but I had no idea there was drama tied to it."

"How do you know Natalia?" Kate asked.

"I don't really know her," Reina responded. "I met her recently and was just curious."

"I think you'll like her. She's a lot like you."

Reina bit back her retort. She was nothing like Natalia and could not believe Kate would actually say something like this to her.

But she wasn't going to correct her friend. There was no need to. She would just keep an eye on Natalia herself.

****

Reina was thrilled when Frankie invited her to attend a birthday party for the oldest member of Bright Hope. She guessed that their little talk at church had helped and now, Frankie trusted her.

She was one of the first to arrive, so that gave her a moment to chat with Frankie.

"I have an idea for the scholarship fund," she told Frankie, as they stood outside in the backyard where they would all have lunch. "We could host a fashion show. I have a friend who is a wonderful designer and I know she'll be more than happy to work with us."

Frankie tilted her head as she considered the idea. "Would it just be the fashion show or would we be providing food as well?"

"I think we should provide lunch."

She nodded. "Let me think about it. It's a good idea, but a lot to take on within a short period of time." Before Reina could say another word, Frankie turned toward the door. "Our guest of honor is here," she said.

Reina's gaze followed Frankie as she walked to greet the guests arriving and Reina's head reared back just a bit. She was not prepared to see Mike's widow in attendance with her daughter.

Charlotte spotted her and before Reina could get away, she stood in front of her. "If I had known you would be here, I wouldn't have come," she stated.

"I'm a close friend of the family," Reina responded. "And I'm a member of Bright Hope. Why wouldn't I be here?"

She sent Leah off to play with some of the other children. "It's just as well," Charlotte said once they were alone. "I've been meaning to have a conversation with you."

"About what?" Reina asked, not able to imagine why Charlotte would want to talk to her.

"About my husband."

Was this woman ever going to leave this alone? "You really don't want to do this here," Reina stated. Lowering her voice, she added, "I know you're grieving, Charlotte, but there is nothing we have to discuss."

"I'm not stupid, Reina," she stated flatly. "I know all about your affair. I also know that Michael left the church to be with you."

Reina shook her head. "You're wrong. When Mike left, I was still in Raleigh. You really shouldn't be saying stuff like this, especially since you don't know what you're talking about."

"You think you're so smart, but you're not," Charlotte hissed. "You joined him in Florida and I don't know what happened between you two, but he didn't deserve to end up dead. Another thing…I know that he didn't kill himself. My husband has always hated taking pills of any kind. So that is not the way that he would've chosen to commit suicide."

Reina gave her a hard stare. "So what are you saying?"

Charlotte stared right back. "Mike was murdered." She paused as if she wanted to give Reina time to digest those words. "And I'm going to find a way to prove it."

"So now you're playing the loyal wife?"

"Excuse me?"

"You're doing all of this now that Mike's dead. Where were you when he needed you?" Before Charlotte could respond, Reina continued, "He made excuses for you when you weren't at church, but everyone knew that you were addicted to pain pills after your back surgery."

Charlotte folded her arms across her chest. "Mike and I had our problems, but I never stopped loving my husband, even while he was cheating on me with some of the women in the congregation." She let a silent second pass. "Surely you knew that you weren't the only one."

Reina pulled her off to a vacant area in the yard where they would not be overheard. "I won't deny that Mike and I were friends," she stated. "I'm sorry he's gone, but maybe you should find a way to move on. Focusing on something that never happened is not healthy." Then, she stabbed Charlotte with, "Oh, and say no to drugs. You have a child depending on you," she said as she glanced across the yard at Leah who was giggling with a group of girls.

Charlotte's body shook in her fury. "You're evil."

"You sound irrational," Reina stated.

Charlotte took a couple of deep breaths and then said, "You better watch your back. Because if I find out that you had something to do with Mike's death, I'm going to make sure you pay."

Reina chuckled. "You're grieving, so I'm going to ignore your pathetic attempt at threatening me.."

"Is everything okay over here?" Traynor inquired as he stepped through the doorway.

"Yes, it's fine," Reina answered. With her eyes on Charlotte, she said, "We were just talking about Pastor Mike."

Traynor gave them both a long glance, nodded, and then stepped back inside.

Charlotte waited until they were alone once again before she said, "I can't wait until he finds out just how good a liar you are." Charlotte paused before she added, "Pastor Deveraux will drop you like a hot potato."

Reina laughed. "Once again you're wrong. I'm not interested in the pastor that way. He's like a father to me. I wasn't having an affair with your husband and I'm not sleeping with Traynor either." She shook her head and looked at Charlotte with pity in her eyes. "You really need help, and I hope you get it. Because all of this talk is getting irritating and my patience is wearing thin."

"I don't care anything about your patience. I'm just telling you that I'm going to find out what really happened to my husband and if you had anything to do with it...."

Reina gave Charlotte a hard stare. "I'm tired of this

and I'm tired of you. So, if you don't stay away from me, I promise you will be very sorry." Then, she turned her back to Charlotte and walked away.

For the rest of the afternoon, Charlotte stayed in one part of the yard while Reina was in another. But the entire time, Reina kept her eyes on Charlotte. Every time she saw her in deep conversation, she wondered if Charlotte was repeating her suspicions about her and Mike.

She was going to have to do something about Charlotte, she decided.

Charlotte's presence had taken away all of the joy of being at the party, so right after lunch, Reina prepared to leave. But Frankie stopped her before she could get through the door.

It was because of her conversation with Charlotte that had Reina's guard up.

But then, Reina relaxed when Frankie said, "I really like the idea of the fashion show to raise funds for our scholarship fund. Would you like to chair the event?"

"I would love it," she responded happily. "I'll get a proposal to you."

Her joy dissipated, though as she walked to her car. She was sure that once Charlotte found out, she wouldn't be happy about this.

That shrew will do anything to try and ruin this for me—but I'm not going to let her, she vowed. No matter what I have to do.

****

"I'm really worried about Charlotte," Reina commented as she applied a spray sheen to Kate's freshly permed hair. "She's been acting a little weird lately."

"She seems fine to me," Kate responded. "She's upset over losing Pastor Mike, which is understandable."

"I don't know." Reina shook her head. " I think something more's going on with her."

Looking at Reina through the mirror, Kate asked, "Like what?"

"Well, when I saw Charlotte at church last week, she seemed a little off. Like she was high on something. Then, at Pastor Deveraux's house, I had a brief conversation with her, but she was hard to understand. Her voice was a little slurred," Reina lied.

"I think her doctor gave her something to ease her nerves," Kate said, still watching Reina in the mirror.

Reina nodded. "Maybe that's it. But I think we should probably keep an eye on her."

Kate bit her bottom lip. "Maybe I should give her a call when I get home—just to check on her."

Reina agreed. "You should because I'm really worried that losing her husband has been too much for her."

By the time Kate stood up from Reina's chair, Kate was convinced that there was something wrong with the past First Lady. Reina was pleased. That's exactly what she had to do. She had to discredit Charlotte just in case she began spewing rumors around the church about her and Mike. She had to make everyone wonder if Charlotte was back on drugs.

This won't be too hard, Reina thought as she watched Kate hurry out of the salon. She had just convinced Kate and after a few more conversations like the one they just had, Kate would start spreading the word. No one would ever know that the rumor began with Reina.

****

Chrissy walked out of the hair store with her purchase, and headed to her car. She checked her watch to see if she still had time to grab something to eat before her lunch hour ended.

"I hope you didn't waste money on that beauty store hair."

She looked around to find Reina sitting in the vehicle next to where she parked.

"What I do with my money is no business of yours," she responded.

Reina got out of her car. "Do you always have such a sour attitude?"

Looking her up and down, Chrissy asked, "Who are you now? Dr. Phil?"

She laughed. "I'm sorry, I forgot your name."

"I'm glad," Chrissy responded. "There's no need for you to know it. We aren't friends."

"We could be," Reina stated. "I think we may have a lot in common."

Chrissy shook her head. "I don't think so."

Reina shrugged. "How is your friend? The one with the split ends."

At first, she was going to ignore that nasty comment. But then she answered, "Sabrina's doing well." Chrissy turned the ignition. "Now if you'll excuse me, I have somewhere to be."

"Don't let me stand in your way."

Chrissy responded, "I won't."

As she pulled off, Chrissy studied Reina in her rear view mirror. *That woman is crazy,* she thought to herself. Even though she was yards away from her, a strange feeling washed over her. A chill snaked down her spine.

She shuddered and turned out of the parking lot, hoping that she'd never have to see that woman again.

****

On the fourth Sunday of every month, Bright Hope hosted a potluck after church to welcome new members and present an opportunity for everyone to get to know one another.

Reina and Kate filled the cups with drinks and as one pitcher emptied, Reina turned to Kate. "Can you bring out another pitcher of lemonade?"

"Sure."

When Kate stepped away, Reina reached into her purse. With a slow glance around the room she made sure that there were no eyes on her as she slipped a clear liquid in the cup in front of her. Then, she tucked her purse away and searched the dining room for Charlotte. She saw her, sitting with a couple of women near the table where Traynor and his family were dining.

"Here you are," Kate said, carrying a fresh pitcher of lemonade.

Reina held up the cup. "Kate, why don't you take this over to Charlotte?" she suggested. "It doesn't look like she has anything to drink."

That was true. Charlotte wanted to stay as far away as possible from Reina, she knew that. That's why Charlotte had never once ventured over to the beverage table. However, Charlotte trusted Kate.

A smile spread across her face when Charlotte accepted the cup of lemonade. Now all she had to do was wait for the drug to take effect.

She didn't have to wait long.

Within minutes, Charlotte began laughing loudly. The women sitting with her looked bewildered.

"Kate," Reina said, as Charlotte's laughter got even louder, "maybe you should go check on her."

"She seemed fine before." Kate shook her head as if she couldn't figure out what was going on.

"It doesn't look as if she's fine now."

"I'll go over there."

Reina watched Kate walk quickly to the other side of the room, then lean over as if she were asking Charlotte if she was okay.

"I'm fine," Charlotte said, loud enough for even Reina to hear. " I wish people would stop asking me that.

All you busybodies in the church—I'm fine."

Reina stayed behind the beverage table and watched the reactions. It was Traynor's table that she studied the most. Traynor looked stunned and she watched Frankie whisper something to Holt before she stood and walked over to the table.

When Frankie leaned over, Charlotte tried to stand up, swaying in her attempt.

While everyone else in the room was concerned, Reina bit back her laughter.

"I don't need help," Charlotte slurred. "It's these whores in the church that are doing this to me." She pointed to one of the women sitting at her table. "Don't think I didn't see how you was eyeing my husband. Now you sitting here in my face."

Charlotte picked up her plate and tossed the food on the woman. "Whore," she spat.

The room gasped collectively.

Charlotte's gaze traveled to Reina. "There's another whore over there. She left town with Mike. She's the reason he's dead."

Reina kept her expression blank.

Traynor stood up, clearing his throat loudly. "She is obviously in need of prayer. C'mon everybody. Let's gather around our dear sister and pray."

"I don't want prayer," Charlotte shouted. "Just leave me alone," she cried.

That was quite a show, Reina thought. She silently congratulated herself for coming up with the idea. As everyone gathered around Charlotte, Reina remained in place and smiled. Even though most heads were bowed and most eyes were closed, there were some who were still staring at Charlotte and Reina knew that as soon as this potluck was over, people would be talking.

It was so perfect.

Chapter 14

"How is Charlotte doing?" Traynor asked when Frankie entered the house. He had gone to their home to wait with Holt and Junior.

"When I was left, she was sleeping." Frankie sat down on the sofa beside her husband. "She was under the influence of something," she said, shaking her head. "We couldn't get her to go to the hospital, but Kate is staying with her tonight."

Traynor shook his head sadly. "She has taken Mike's death harder than I thought."

Frankie agreed. "She really believes that he cheated on her with members of the congregation."

"She named Reina," Holt stated.

"Do you think it's true?" Frankie asked.

"It is not our place to judge," Traynor responded before Holt could.

Frankie said anyway, "If Charlotte is right, it certainly does paint a different picture of Reina."

"We shouldn't be too harsh with her," Holt

commented. "We are all flawed individuals."

"And, we don't know if what Charlotte said was true. Clearly she was high."

"I understand all that, but I have to be honest, if Charlotte is right, I wouldn't be comfortable around Reina knowing that she's a home wrecker. That's not the kind of friend I want in my circle."

"Like I said, Charlotte is sick, so we don't really know what to believe," Traynor said.

"We can always ask Reina," Frankie suggested. "I'm just not sure she'd be honest about it, though."

"Let's focus on taking care of Charlotte," Traynor said. "She's the one who needs us right now and the rest of that – it's none of our business."

"You're right, Pop," Frankie responded. "I'm going back to check on her tomorrow morning. I told Kate I'd come over around ten."

The conversation shifted to furniture Traynor was considering buying for his house, but Frankie's thoughts stayed on Reina. Like she'd just told her husband and father-in-law, if Reina had been messing around with Mike before he died, then she was not the type of friend Frankie wanted.

She was glad that she had discernment and Frankie trusted that God would reveal the truth to her in time.

****

"I'd like to speak to someone about my husband,"

Charlotte said. She had finally summoned up her courage to do what she'd wanted to do for a while now. She'd driven to the police station after dropping Leah off at school.

"What is this about, ma'am?" the officer behind the counter asked. Even though he spoke to her, his head was still lowered as he jotted something down on a pad.

"My husband is Pastor Michael Jennings and I believe he was murdered."

The officer looked up. "Murdered? By who?"

"That's just it," Charlotte responded. "I don't know. They found him dead in an apartment in Florida. The police there said it was suicide, but I don't believe it."

The officer studied her for just a moment. "Just have a seat over there and someone will be with you shortly."

Charlotte did as instructed. As she sat on the edge of the chair, she prayed that the truth would be revealed.

Twenty minutes passed before a tall man in plain clothes walked out. "I'm Detective Jacobs. How can I help you?"

Charlotte introduced herself. "My husband was Pastor Mike Jennings and I believe he was killed."

He nodded. "We can talk in my office," he said.

Charlotte followed him down a long hallway to a small office. There were a couple of pictures on the wall, but those photos did nothing to enhance the room's dreary atmosphere. She clutched her purse tightly in her hands as she sat down in one of the empty chairs.

The detective said, "I knew your husband, Mrs.

Jennings."

"You did?" she said, clutching the strap of her purse tightly.

"Not personally, but I knew him from the community and I'd attended your church a few times."

Charlotte nodded.

"That's why when this first happened, I wanted to know for myself. So, I called and spoke with a detective that handled the case in Florida," he stated. He waited a moment before he added, "Mrs. Jennings, there was no evidence of foul play."

"But Michael didn't like taking pills of any kind," Charlotte told him.

"Even with that, I'm afraid there isn't anything we can do, Mrs. Jennings. Your husband's death was ruled a suicide."

She felt tears spilling from her eyes and she wiped them away. "I know that he wouldn't kill himself."

"He had left town, he was using an alias," Detective Jacobs said. "Do you know if he was in some sort of trouble?"

"He stole money from the church," Charlotte said softly. "That's all I know."

"I heard about the money," the detective said. "Did your husband gamble?"

"No," she responded. Then, after thinking about it for another moment, she added, "Not that I was aware of, anyway."

He nodded.

She took a deep breath before she added, "He was having an affair, though."

The detective nodded again. "When things like this happen, it's been my experience that he may have been in trouble and felt there was no way out. I'm sorry for your loss, Mrs. Jennings. But like I said, there is nothing more that we can do."

She sat still for a few more seconds, swallowing the despair in her throat. Then she said, "Thank you," before she stood to leave. When Charlotte left the police station, she considered that the detective might be right, but her spirit remained unsettled.

****

"Charlotte, it's so good to see you," Natalia said as she embraced her friend. "I didn't think you were coming to the tea." She felt guilty for not reaching out to Charlotte earlier, but her focus had been on planning the charity event. Not to mention that Natalia had stayed far away, not knowing how close Charlotte was to Traynor.

Natalia had known Charlotte from the days when her husband was the youth pastor at Natalia's father's church. She didn't consider the two of them best friends, but they were close enough that Natalia now wished that she had reached out sooner.

"I thought being here with all of you would help some," she responded, shivering. "I can't sit home because it reminds me of Michael. I can't believe he's gone, but I have to find a way to get on with my life."

Natalia held Charlotte's shaking body in her arms. "I'm so sorry about everything."

"Thank you, Natalia," she mumbled into her friend's shoulder.

They embraced once more.

"Let's join everyone in the living room," Natalia suggested.

She noted how her friend trembled and that disturbed her. Then, Natalia watched as she engaged with the others. Charlotte seemed friendly enough, but something was off. Especially since she couldn't stop trembling.

Natalia had heard about Charlotte's rant at church last Sunday from Kate. She worried that Charlotte was back on the pills again and she felt so bad for her friend. She couldn't imagine losing the love of your life. Losing her parents had been hard enough.

Thankfully, the tea had gone smoothly. There were no outbursts and no one said anything to insult Charlotte with the rumors that had been circulating about her. Natalia was glad that Charlotte lingered behind as the other women began to leave. And finally, it was just the two of them.

"I honestly don't remember much about Sunday," Charlotte told her after Natalia questioned her about what she'd heard. "Natalia, I'm so embarrassed. I'm not going to church tomorrow because I can't face anyone."

"I'm so sorry," Natalia uttered as she took her friend's hand in hers.

"The only thing I can think of is that I was drugged somehow."

"So, you didn't take any medication?"

Charlotte shook her head. "No! Not at all." And then she paused and after a thoughtful moment, she said, "At least I don't think I did." She covered her face with her hands. "I don't know, Natalia," she cried.

Rubbing her back, Natalia asked, "Well, maybe it wasn't pills. Maybe it was something you ate...or drank."

"I don't know how it could be. Everyone ate the same food. It was a potluck and all I had to drink was lemonade."

After a couple of thoughtful seconds, Natalia said, "You know what? I don't think it's such a good idea for you to be alone right now."

Charlotte nodded. "I don't think so either, but I don't know what to do. I don't have anywhere to go. And I have Leah."

"Why don't you and Leah come stay with me for a while? This house is certainly big enough."

Charlotte looked up. Her eyes were wet with tears when she asked, "Are you sure that you wouldn't mind?"

"Of course not, I'd love to have you. I'd love the company, to be honest."

"Oh, thank you so much," she said, and hugged her friend in gratitude. "I'm so unsure about everything that I don't even trust myself with Leah." She sat back. "This will help me get myself together." She was quiet for a few moments, as if there were many thoughts on her mind, but she wasn't sure what she should share. Finally, she said, "Natalia, I hope that you don't think I'm crazy, but I don't believe for one second that Michael committed suicide. He loved himself too much for that. I think he was murdered."

"By who?" Natalia said, trying to act like she was really considering what Charlotte had to say. But she didn't believe her friend. The police had been all over that case. They would know what happened to Mike.

"I have someone in mind, but I just don't have any proof."

"So what are you going to do?" Natalia asked. She didn't want to really encourage her friend; Natalia was sure that Charlotte's theory could possibly be because of the drugs that she might be taking.

"I went to the police, but they just treated me like a grieving widow in denial. I even told them that Michael was having an affair, but they still refused to do anything about it." She paused. "And then, there's this other thing, the money."

"What about it?"

"Mike took fifty thousand dollars from the church."

"I heard about that. I was hoping that it was just a rumor," Natalia said.

Charlotte shook her head. "Not a rumor, it's true. But no one has said anything about the money. The detectives in Florida didn't mention it and the detective today didn't say anything either."

"Did you ask about it?"

"No. But if they'd found it, wouldn't the police have said something?"

Natalia nodded, though inside she thought, Not necessarily. The police could have kept the money. But Natalia didn't say a word. She just let her friend continue with her theories.

"And, he was using a fake name." Charlotte shook her head and spoke strongly and clearly when she said, "This was not the man that I knew and loved."

It was because of the way that she spoke, that Natalia asked, "Are you sure about all of this, Charlotte?"

She nodded. "No money was found, he was using an alias, he wouldn't have committed suicide, at least not with pills. And oh, he was involved with this hairstylist. And she's still here, tormenting me. Now she's hanging around Traynor Deveraux and his family."

Charlotte's words prompted Natalia to ask, "What's her name?"

"Reina Cannon."

Natalia nodded slowly. "I've met her."

"Stay away from her, Natalia. She is evil." Charlotte paused for a moment. "You know something...this just came to me. You asked if I'd had anything to eat or drink before all of that stuff happened on Sunday."

"Yeah..." Natalia frowned. "What are you thinking?"

Charlotte paused and shook her head as if she couldn't believe the thoughts that she was having. "I drank some lemonade."

"Yeah, you said that."

"From the beverage table."

Natalia frowned. Was her friend losing it again? Everyone in that place had probably had lemonade from the beverage table.

"I didn't get it myself," Charlotte continued. "Kate gave it to me. From the table…where Reina was working."

Together, they were silent, but when they looked up, each could tell that they had the same thought.

"Are you sure?" Natalia felt ice spreading through her veins. She didn't really know Reina, but she'd known all along that she didn't trust that woman.

Charlotte nodded. "I didn't go over there because I didn't want to deal with Reina. I wouldn't have accepted it if Kate hadn't been the one to bring me the lemonade."

Natalia was pensive for a moment. "It's possible that Reina could have slipped something in your drink and had Kate bring it to you. Do you remember if she were ever alone? Did she have time to do that?"

"As far as I know, Kate was with her the entire time," Charlotte responded. "But something happened. Now that I really think about it, I promise you I didn't take anything." Her eyes filled with tears. "You believe me, don't you?"

"I believe you." Natalia reached over and covered Charlotte's hand with her own.

"And I promise you, if Reina is responsible for what happened to you and Mike—I'll find out."

"Really? You're willing to help me?"

"Yes. I never trusted Reina, from the moment I met her."

Charlotte's body sagged with relief. "Thank you, Natalia."

"Go home and pack some clothes for you and Leah. Where's she now?"

"She's with my mom."

"We'll pack a few things, pick her up and when you two get back here, we'll figure something out."

Charlotte rushed off as if she were eager to return. And when she left, Natalia went into her home office, turned on the computer, sat down and began searching for information on Reina Cannon.

She was disappointed when nothing of substance came back. The woman did not even have a Facebook or Twitter account. Not even for her hair salon. Reina had a website for her business, but other than that, there was no other information on her.

Natalia Googled her own name and found several sites with general information and a few articles. Just as she suspected – every business person had some kind of Internet footprint these days.

Puzzled, she got up and left her desk. It was suspicious, but Natalia knew that there were people who guarded their personal information off the Internet. She knew enough about Reina to know that she was probably one of those people.

The ringing phone interrupted her thoughts.

"You were on my mind," Dean said, the moment she

answered, "so I wanted to give you a call."

She smiled. "I'm glad you did."

"Something wrong?" he asked.

"Not with me. I have a friend who's going through a lot right now. I invited her to stay with me for a while."

"That's nice of you."

"I don't think she needs to be alone." Natalia changed the subject. "I don't want to talk about her. I enjoyed our time together last night."

"So did I," Dean responded.

It had been several weeks now and she and Dean had been on dozens of dates. And each time, she enjoyed their time together even more.

"I'd planned to cook dinner for you this weekend, but my friend and her daughter will be here."

"You're welcome to cook at my place," he suggested. "I'll even help."

She smiled. "That's a plan."

They discussed the menu and the time she'd meet him before they hung up. She was still smiling when she reached over a picked up the photograph of her father. "I met someone," she told him. "I'm not sure how things are going to go, but he seems nice." She chuckled. "I'm sure you're not surprised. You always said that I'd marry a preacher or an attorney. Turns out he's both."

She kissed the frame. "I miss you, Daddy." Natalia did the same with the photo of her mother. "I miss you, Mommy. I promised you that I would look out for Daddy and I kept that promise as best I could."

For the first time in a long time, she felt good talking to her parents. She checked her watch, then went upstairs to freshen the room where she would put Charlotte and her daughter. She looked forward to having some company and she was glad that she could help her friend.

She was still not quite convinced about Mike's death being a murder, but Reina's involvement certainly raised some questions. And if Charlotte was right about Reina— she found it hard to digest that Traynor would allow someone so sinister so close to his family.

But then again, he had been married to Jessie Belle.

Natalia wasn't sure if Charlotte confided in him because she didn't mention if she had. She made a mental note to ask her when she returned. Traynor deserved to know if Reina was dangerous.

****

Reina settled back against the cushions of her sofa with a huge box. She opened it to reveal a stack of articles, photos, and documents.

She picked up her birth certificate, which listed her birthplace as Richmond, Georgia. Her eyes strayed to the name of her mother and stayed there. If only this were the truth.

Gloria Jean Ricks was not her birth mother, although she was listed as such. Henry Ricks was definitely not her father. He was nothing but a pervert who had stolen her virginity when she was only twelve while Gloria did nothing, even after he impregnated her at fifteen. Her son died shortly after he was born.

The sexual abuse ended when Gloria and Henry died in a house fire six months later. Thankfully, she was not home at the time.

It was not until she had given birth to her son that she found out they were not her biological parents. She had overheard them arguing late one night. It was then that she found out what Gloria did when she left home at all odd hours. This was when Reina learned the tragic story of her birth.

Her teen mother had come to Gloria for an abortion, but her pregnancy was advanced to the point that an abortion was life threatening. The girl's mother did not want the child and was willing to take the risks to free her daughter of the baby.

However, Gloria didn't perform an abortion. She gave the girl something to induce labor and delivered the baby. At thirty-something weeks, no one really expected her to live, but Reina entered the world with a strong will to survive.

For reasons, Reina would never understand, Gloria decided to make the child her own, condemning Reina to a life of hell. It would have been much better to die. It was in that moment when she learned the truth, that Reina decided she had no more use for Henry and Gloria Ricks.

After their deaths, Reina searched to find her biological mother. It wasn't an easy task until she learned about Gloria's safe deposit box, the contents of which were now in the box she held on her lap along with her own personal collection of information she'd gathered over the years—information on her mother and the man she suspected to be her father. From information she'd put together, her parents had been high school sweethearts, but he'd died a few years before she began her search. He'd played pro football for a few years before his cancer diagnosis that eventually killed him. She doubted he ever knew anything about her.

Her mother loved her father, but people were not accepting of a white man and black woman as a couple in those days. Reina wanted to believe that if they could have been together—her life would have turned out much differently.

When she began her search, Reina figured that her mother had no idea that the child she bore was still very much alive. She expected that when her mother found out, she would welcome her long-lost daughter with open arms, but that was not the case. The woman rejected her.

That was fine, though. Because Reina had figured out a way to get everything that she'd always wanted.

There was just one problem though...Charlotte. Something had to be done about her and Reina knew exactly what to do.

****

Reina sprinted up the ghostly street to the cul-de-sac where Charlotte's house was located in a North Raleigh neighborhood not far from where she lived. She wiped her brow to remove the small beads of sweat that had accumulated in her quest to move around undetected.

As she approached the house, Reina saw the headlights of a SUV creeping up the deserted street. She released a sigh of relief as the vehicle sped up and then continued past the driveway.

The SUV came to a sudden stop in front of the house next door. A puff of gray smoke produced a faint shadow and the scent of burnt rubber bit into the night. A teenage boy jumped out of the driver's seat and rushed up to the door.

Reina stopped in her tracks, hidden by a large tree on the side of Charlotte's house. She did not move or make a sound until the boy had disappeared into the house.

Reina used the key that she had taken off of Mike's key ring to unlock the door. When she'd taken his key, she had no plans to use it; she'd taken it just in case. She eased inside, surveyed the entryway, and then waited in the living room.

She didn't have long to wait.

Just a few minutes after she'd arrived, Charlotte rushed in, looking agitated. She navigated to the staircase, then stopped suddenly and looked into the living room. She gasped.

"What are you doing in my house?" Charlotte demanded.

She was trying hard not to show fear, but Reina was not fooled by her weak attempt at bravado. "You've been spreading rumors about me, Charlotte and I don't like it."

Charlotte walked briskly across the hardwood floor, her heels making tapping sounds to the steady rhythm of her movement. "I want you out of here right now."

"I'll leave when I'm good and ready."

She reached for the telephone. "I'm calling the police."

"I don't think so," Reina stated as she rushed to her feet. "Because then I'd have to tell them all about the drugs that you keep in the house. I'm sure you don't want your daughter being raised in foster care."

"Drugs ..." Charlotte looked confused. "Why do you keep talking about drugs? I don't have any drugs here."

Reina held up a plastic bag containing several bottles of medication.

"Those aren't mine," she replied, though her voice trembled.

"They have your name on them."

Charlotte frowned, then her eyes widened in understanding. "Why are you doing this to me? You wanted Michael and he chose you. Why are you coming after me now?"

She shrugged. "Mike and I were really good together in the beginning, but then he had this stupid idea that we needed to run away together and start over," Reina stated. "I didn't want to leave Raleigh. But I had to go because Mike would not leave unless I agreed to go with him. And I needed him out of Raleigh."

"Why?" Charlotte asked, though her eyes darted

around the room as if she were looking for something.

"I had my reasons – they're not important," Reina said, closing the space between them.

Now, Charlotte glanced toward the door, then back at Reina. "So, you went with him to Florida and then, what happened? What did you do?"

"You ask a lot of questions," Reina said.

Charlotte continued, "Did you take the money that he had from the church?"

She gave Charlotte a sugary smile.. "I'm not sure what you mean."

Her voice had drifted to almost a hushed whisper. "Did you kill him?"

She paused for just a moment. "Charlotte, don't ask questions that you're not ready to hear the answer to, because I won't lie to you."

Her eyes filled with tears. "Did you kill my husband?"

Looking her straight in the eyes, Reina said, "I didn't want to spend the rest of my life tied down to a man I didn't love. I knew that Mike wasn't going to just let me go." Reina kept her eyes on Charlotte's horrified gaze. "He loved me too much."

"Noooo ..." Charlotte shook her head as she sank down on the sofa as if she could no longer stand.

Reina paced in front of her.. "It's important that you understand that I wasn't trying to take your husband away from you, Charlotte. I simply wanted him out of the way. The church needed a new pastor and disgracing Mike was the only way we would get one."

Charlotte stiffened in shock. "You did this so that you could get Pastor Deveraux to take over? Why?"

"I had my reasons."

"You're sick!"

"No, that would be you, Charlotte." Reina pulled a needle out of her pocket. "You're very sick and it's time to end your suffering. You love Mike so much, now you can join him."

Slowly, Charlotte stood. She held her hands up, and taking tiny steps, she backed out of the room. "Don't do this...I have a daughter...I won't tell anybody what you just told me," she cried. "Please just leave. I'm the only parent my little girl has left...."

"She'll be fine. I promise. Your mother will be there for Leah."

Charlotte lurched to the side, reached for the vase on the living room table and flung it at Reina. For a moment, she was caught off-guard. But then as the vase crashed to the floor, Reina laughed. "Don't fight this, Charlotte. I'm just giving you what you want. Peace."

Screaming, Charlotte ran to the front door, but her hands trembled and she fumbled with the lock. Before she could get the door open, Reina grabbed her, and jammed the needle into her forearm.

Charlotte twisted and turned, trying to fend Reina off. But Reina was much stronger and the drug in the syringe was already working.

Charlotte moaned as her limbs went limp. "Dear God...my baby...."

Holding her by her waist, Reina struggled, but managed to get Charlotte onto the sofa. And when she laid her back, Charlotte was like a noodle.

"Go to sleep, Charlotte," Reina whispered in a soothing tone. "I won't leave your side until the end."

Charlotte's eyes fluttered as she fought to keep them open.

Reina said, "You may not believe this, but I didn't want this to happen. I really didn't, but you just couldn't shut up."

Charlotte's eyes closed.

"I can't let anyone interfere with my plans."

It only took a few minutes before Charlotte stopped breathing.

Reina laid her down gently on the sofa. She was glad that Leah was with her grandmother so that she would not have to witness this tragedy.

Outside, she quickened her retreat and stumbled on the sidewalk. But then she steadied herself, though she didn't slow her steps. She ran frantically down the street toward the rental car she had driven.

****

Reina stepped out of the shower and dried her body with a fluffy towel. She stared at her reflection in the mirror and attempted a confident smile, but her bottom lip quivered and her eyes watered slightly.

"Keep it together," she told herself. "You've done

this before."

A thick drop of sweat trickled down her chest and settled at the top of her towel. Even though she'd taken a shower, she couldn't stop sweating. And she couldn't stop the thoughts of Charlotte and how her body felt as life ebbed out of it.

It frustrated her that she'd had to improvise. Doing that to Charlotte wasn't part of the plan.

Why couldn't Charlotte have just kept her mouth shut?

Reina felt bad, but there was nothing else that she could have done. She'd had no choice.

Chapter 15

Natalia gasped in shock as she read the newspaper. She couldn't believe what she was reading.

I just talked to Charlotte. She was supposed to come back to my house.

Natalia had called her twice last night and left a couple of messages, but she had assumed that Charlotte had gone to her mother's house. She fully expected to hear from her today.

Why would she do this?

She read the article once again, but Natalia didn't believe the words. "She didn't commit suicide," she whispered. "Charlotte would never leave her daughter like this."

Natalia recalled how upset she'd been, but even with that, she wouldn't do this. So if she didn't kill herself, then what happened?

An image of Reina floated across her mind as she remembered all the revelations that Charlotte had shared with her about Reina. But she had no proof.

Still, Natalia was determined to find out what happened to Charlotte. If Reina were responsible, then she would gladly see that she spent the rest of her life in prison. But what could her motive be? Why would she torment Charlotte and then kill her? Why would she kill Mike?

Natalia once again considered everything that Charlotte told her and the more she thought about it, the more it didn't make sense. Maybe Mike had committed suicide and Charlotte blamed Reina. Or maybe Reina blamed Charlotte.

She couldn't get any of this to make sense.

The first thing she needed to do was find out exactly what happened to Mike. She'd start there and maybe that would give her some answers. She picked up her phone, and then paused. Maybe she shouldn't do this alone. Maybe she should ask Dean to help her.

But she pushed that thought out of her mind. She and Dean were just becoming closer and she didn't want to mess up their relationship or put him in any kind of danger. She dialed the number and made airline reservations just for herself for a flight to Florida the following week. She would have left that night, but she couldn't leave before the funeral. She had to be here for Charlotte's mother and Leah.

Leah. That poor baby, she thought. She had to get to the bottom of this for that little girl who had now lost both of her parents to suicide.

Or maybe neither one of them committed suicide.

Could Reina really be a murderer?

Natalia was determined to find out and if she found enough evidence, she was going straight to the police. And after that, she'd warn Traynor.

The thought that Reina might come after her, entered her mind, but Natalia would not let that frighten her. Jessie Belle was pure evil, but if Reina murdered her friends, then she was evil personified. That trumped all of her fear.

Natalia vowed not to return until she discovered the truth.

****

"Remember the pastor that committed suicide down in Florida," Chrissy began the moment that Sabrina arrived home.

"Yeah," she responded as she took off her coat. "He was the former pastor at Bright Hope where Pastor Deveraux is preaching."

"They just found his wife dead of a drug overdose. The article says that she committed suicide, too."

Sabrina dropped down on the sofa. "What in the world is going on? The devil is truly busy."

"Did you know them?" Chrissy asked.

Shaking her head, Sabrina responded, "No. I thought about checking out his church, but I never did. I think my cousin was friends with her when their husbands worked together as pastors."

"It's really sad," Chrissy stated.

Sabrina agreed, but then, with a sigh asked, "So, how was your day?"

"It was okay," Chrissy said, glad that Sabrina changed the subject. "We weren't that busy."

"Have you decided if you're going to get your real estate license?" Sabrina asked.

"I'm seriously considering it," she responded. "The only thing that's stopping me now is my arrest record. I have a couple of them and that might come back to haunt me."

"I'm sure there are other people with that license who've been arrested," Sabrina said waving Chrissy's words away with her hand. "Just give it to the Lord."

Chrissy's mouth tightened, but she did not say anything. She was not in the mood for a mini sermon about having faith in a loving God.

Sabrina strolled into the kitchen and began pulling out food from the refrigerator. "We have some leftover spaghetti."

"That's fine," she responded. "I want you to show me how to make the garlic bread."

Sabrina stopped in her tracks. "Did I just hear you correctly? You want to actually make something?"

"I don't know about you, but I don't intend to live with you forever," Chrissy said with a tiny smile. "It's time I learn how to cook."

Sabrina's eyes were tear bright, but she kept her composure. "Grab the French bread and the garlic butter."

"I think I can handle that," she said with a short laugh.

It didn't take them long to put their meal together and Chrissy smiled with pride when the garlic bread came out of the oven a golden brown.

"It's perfect," Sabrina told her. "Great job."

"I'm motivated. What can I do now?" Chrissy asked.

"Make the salad," Sabrina said as she handed her a tomato.

They ate dinner and watched a couple of movies before retiring to their bedrooms. When Chrissy was alone, she recalled Sabrina's words.

Just give it to the Lord.

With those words playing in her head, she reached over to her nightstand, picked up the Bible and placed it upright in her lap. Chrissy closed her eyes, then she let the book fall open.

Opening her eyes, she peered at the page.

She moaned softly as she read the verse.

Repent, then, and turn to God, so that your sins may be wiped out, that times of refreshing may come from the Lord....

Chrissy re-read the verse, but she knew that these words weren't true about her.. You can't forgive me, she said in her mind to God. You know my thoughts. How could You forgive me when I feel the way I do?

Chrissy was never going to change. Because of that, she knew that she'd never have a real relationship with

God.

****

Just as Reina grabbed a plate of food, Natalia stepped in front of her.

Reina had not expected to see her here, at Charlotte's services. Actually, she hadn't seen her during the funeral, so that's why she was so shocked to see her at the repast. She had no idea that Charlotte and Natalia even knew each other. Raleigh was clearly not as large as she thought.

"I know that you and Charlotte weren't friends," Natalia spoke first, "so tell me, Reina, do you make it a habit of attending funerals of people that you have no relationship with?"

"I could ask you the same thing, Natalia. Charlotte and I may not have been friends, but at least we were members of the same church."

"Charlotte and I have been friends for years. In fact, I was a bridesmaid at her wedding."

Reina's surprise showed on her face. "Well then, I'm sorry for your loss, Natalia."

"If it were coming out of sincerity, I would thank you. However, I'm not stupid." Natalia lowered her voice. "Charlotte told me all about you and Mike, then she suddenly turns up dead." She waited to see if Reina would respond. When she didn't, Natalia continued, "Consider yourself forewarned, Reina. I'm going to find all of the skeletons in your closet, and when I do…let's just say that you should get used to wearing a gray or an orange prison jumpsuit, sweetie."

Reina smiled, but the warmth of her smile never reached her eyes. "Come and get me. It will be the last thing you ever do in life."

Natalia raised her eyebrows. "Is that a threat?"

At first, Reina didn't respond. She just looked past Natalia. Then, she said, "You might want to make your exit right about now. Traynor's staring you down and he looks pretty angry."

Natalia didn't turn around; she kept her eyes on Reina. "I'm not done with you."

"I disagree. You and I don't any anything to talk about."

Natalia smiled, though there was a warning in her eyes. "Enjoy this moment... while you can." Then she turned around and walked briskly toward the exit doors.

Reina stood with her fists clenched and her eyes filled with tears of frustration. Why was everyone trying to get in her way? Once again, she was going to have to step up her plans.

This was supposed to be so simple, but now there were two people dead.

And the way things were looking, Natalia just might be the third.

****

"Hello, can I speak with the manager, please?" Natalia asked the young girl seated behind the desk in the rental office. She flew to Jacksonville two days after Charlotte's funeral.

The young woman responded, "I'm the assistant manager. Is there something wrong?"

Natalia hadn't worked this whole encounter out in her head. She knew that she might hit a dead end here; no one was supposed to give out the kind of information she was asking for. But she had to try. "I just wanted to talk to someone about the man that was found here a few months ago. The man who died. He was my brother," Natalia lied. "I just want to find out as much as I can about his last days."

"I'm very sorry for your loss, Miss ..."

"It's Mrs. Winters. I'm married." She pulled out her driver's license.

"The manager is currently in a meeting, but I was here that day, although..." She hesitated. "I'm not sure I'm supposed to talk about it."

"Please, this has been very hard on my family."

"I understand," the young woman. "But you can speak with the detective on the case. He can probably tell you everything."

"I...I spoke with him already," Natalia lied once again. "But we need," she lowered her eyes and sniffed before she looked up again, "we want to know about his final hours."

"I'm not sure that I can help you with that."

"I think you can," Natalia pushed. "Please, my family…our mother."

The mention of their fake mother seemed to be the thing that pushed the young girl over to her side. She looked both ways before she said, "We can talk in my office."

"Thank you so much," Natalia said before she followed her down the hall. She knew that she didn't have much time. Once the manager came out, he or she just might shut this meeting down. So the moment they both sat down, Natalia started her questioning right away. "Do you happen to know if Mike lived alone in the apartment?"

Now that the woman agreed to talk to Natalia, she sang like a jailbird. "I used to see him with a woman and I know she stayed there often. She wasn't on the lease, however."

"What did she look like?" Natalia asked.

"She was biracial, I think. She had funny colored eyes—I couldn't quite tell what color they were, and she had gorgeous honey blond hair. Oh yeah, she had this tiny mole on her lip. I noticed it because my son has one on his lip and it reminded me of him."

Reina was here with Mike. Charlotte was right. Reina and Mike were having an affair.

"Did you tell the police about the woman who spent time with him?"

"Yes, they asked that same question."

That was all Natalia needed to know. "I appreciate

you taking the time to talk to me," Natalia said as she rose to her feet. "This has just been a hard time on the family. Our mother," she said again.

Natalia walked out of the office quickly and navigated through the exit doors. She could hardly wait to get back to Raleigh. She still didn't have proof that Mike's death had been a murder, but she was sure that Reina definitely knew more than she was saying. Whatever secrets Reina was holding close to her breast—Natalia planned to expose them all.

****

Frankie handed Reina a bouquet of roses at the end of the fashion show. "You did a wonderful job. Thanks to you, we raised quite a bit of money for the scholarship fund."

"Thank you."

"Okay, you know you're going to have to do this annually now," Frankie told her. "No one feels they can top this event."

Reina laughed. "I love doing stuff like this, so I don't mind at all."

"I loved the way all the women came together. We needed this."

She agreed. "Frankie, thank you for all you've done to bring the women's ministry back to the way it used to be. I hate that Charlotte's gone, but at least some good has come out of it."

"I suppose that's one way to look at it."

The only way Reina saw it—she was carefree, happy and living a life that she dreamed existed. This would not have happened if Charlotte were still alive.

In the weeks since Reina had begun to put together this fashion show, Frankie's son had taken to calling her Auntie, which warmed Reina's soul. It made her feel as if she was a member of the Deveraux family. She and Frankie had even been spending time together outside of church events. She delighted in getting to know her better.

Reina placed her flowers carefully on a chair backstage. She helped one of the women pack up the last of the dresses.

"You did a wonderful job, Reina."

"Thank you, Nancy. I want you to know that I really appreciate your hard work. I couldn't have done it without you."

"If you decide to chair again next year, I'll be happy to help again."

"Okay, I'm going to take you up on it," Reina promised.

She was the last one to leave the banquet hall and when she got outside, she glanced around the parking lot to see if Traynor was still around, but she did not see his car. A wave of disappointment washed over her. Reina thought he would have at least said something to her about the success of the show before he left.

"It's fine," she reassured herself. It wasn't like he had

deserted her or anything. He was probably tired or maybe he just wanted to be alone.

Reina unlocked her car and slipped inside, placing her flowers on the empty passenger seat. She hummed to the music playing on the radio as she drove to her house.

She had never really noticed just how beautiful Raleigh was at night. Spring was almost here, heralded by the increasing temperatures during the day. Reina was looking forward to warmer weather. She loved to travel when the weather was hot. Only this time, she would not be alone.

****

Natalia caught herself staring at Dean.

She couldn't help it. He looked handsome enough to grace the cover of a GQ magazine. But it was his eyes that drew her in. His eyes were a beautiful shade of brown.

He was smiling at her now, and she wondered exactly how long she had been examining his face.

She flushed in embarrassment. "I apologize for staring."

"You don't have to apologize. I was staring at you—I'm sure you hear this all the time, but you are gorgeous."

Natalia smiled. "Thank you."

"I guess we should check out the menu," Dean said with a chuckle.

"We should because I'm hungry."

The server came to check on them.

"Do you know what you want?" Dean inquired.

Natalia nodded. "I'd like the braised beef with garlic mashed potatoes."

He ordered the same.

She could not get over how much she and Dean had in common. He had literally appeared out of nowhere and somehow managed to grip her heart stronger than she would have ever imagined. There was something different about him. He was not like any other man she had ever dated.

He was the perfect gentleman whenever they were together. Dean believed in opening doors for her, bringing her flowers or a book he had heard was great— he was attentive and gave her compliments often.

As much as Natalia wanted to keep her thoughts pure, it just was not happening. Don't rush into anything, she warned herself.

"There's something you need to know," he stated, breaking into her impure thoughts.

She looked up at him. "What is it?"

Dean reached over and took her hand in his. "We've been seeing each other for a while now."

She nodded.

"I want you to know that I'm not looking to have just a girlfriend. I am looking for a wife. I'm ready to settle down."

She sat, bewildered at what to say.

He smiled. "I hope I didn't just scare you away."

"No, you didn't," Natalia responded. "I'm just a little surprised. I haven't dated anyone who wanted a serious relationship. Ever."

"That's because God was preserving you for me," he announced.

She noted the caring tone of his voice and her heart warmed. Natalia wasn't sure why she felt so drawn to him, but maybe Dean was right. Maybe God had kept her just for him.

"I'm looking to settle down as well," she told him. "However, I don't want to rush this relationship, Dean. Let's take our time and really get to know one another. If we end up getting married, then I want it to be for life."

"I can live with that. However, I was hoping to have the wedding next week."

Natalia laughed at him. It felt so good to laugh. She couldn't remember the last time she had.

The server arrived with their food.

She continued to laugh while they ate. For the first time in years, Natalia had hope for the future.

Chapter 16

Traynor went up to the attic to clear out some of the stuff he brought with him from Georgia. He paused when he found a box with Jessie Bell's name scribbled on top. It took him a moment, but he sat down on one of the wing chairs and opened it. Inside, he found mementos from Jessie Belle's youth, school photographs, cards and a couple of journals.

He chuckled at her first grade photo. She was a beauty even then. He pulled out all of the pictures, deciding he would put together an album for Holt. Then, he picked up one of the journals. He hadn't been able to look through the journals when Jessie Belle first died, nor when he'd packed up everything and moved here.

He flipped the first journal open and from the dates written in it, the book contained Jessie Belle's thoughts when she was sixteen.

Although curious, Traynor decided he was not ready to invade her privacy. One day he wanted to get a glimpse into what Jessie Belle was like during her teen years. But not today.

Even though the pictures made him smile, his thoughts turned dark once again as he thought about what happened to his wife.

"Lord, I know what the Word says about vengeance…I have to avenge my Jessie Belle. I wasn't there to protect her and I should have been there. I am going to make sure no one else ever hurts my family again."

He had fantasized many times about ruining Natalia. Every time he saw her, he wanted to wipe that smug look off her face that she always gave him. She was confident that he would remain quiet out of fear that she would sully his reputation. Traynor was to the point that he no longer cared about much of anything anymore. The only reason why he hadn't gone to the police about Natalia was because he didn't have any proof.

Traynor slammed the box on the floor. Give me one good reason why Natalia deserves to live and not Jessie Belle or Mike and Charlotte.

But even though he wanted to hurt her the way she'd hurt him, Traynor was afraid that he might never be able to make Natalia pay. That thought hurt him to his heart.

****

Her relationship with Dean was going well, but there was still Charlotte and her death that rested heavy on her mind.

When Natalia had first returned to Raleigh, she thought about going to the police. But her initial excitement died on the plane ride home and she thought about 'her evidence.' What did she really have? That Reina was in Florida? That was a long way from her being a killer.

Even though she didn't have enough to go to the police, she did have enough for Traynor. That's why she was on her way over to his home. He needed to know the truth about Reina.

She was sure she wouldn't be well received, at least not at first. But once he heard what she had to say, she was sure he'd change his mind about her.

She tried to have confidence as she parked her car and walked up to Traynor's door. But she lost it when she knocked and he opened the door.

"What are you doing here?" Traynor demanded when he found her standing on the porch.

"May I come in?" she asked.

"For what?"

She took a deep breath. "I think there's something you need to know about Reina Cannon," she stated. "She and Pastor Mike were having an affair."

Traynor glared at her. "I think you'd better leave," he said. "I don't want to hear any more of your lies."

"It's not a lie," Natalia retorted. "Charlotte and I are...we were friends. She's the one who told me about the affair, and now she's dead. Charlotte also believed that Mike was murdered."

"Charlotte was distraught after losing her husband," Traynor said in a tone that told Natalia he thought her words were ridiculous. "I'm sure she didn't want to believe that Mike would commit suicide."

"Well, what about the affair?" Natalia asked.

"I don't have any comment about that. I don't know if it's true; I doubt that it is. But whether it is or not, I just don't know why you would come all the way over here to tell me this?"

She paused for a moment, hoping that he would finally invite her into his home. It seemed so cold to be discussing this out in the open. But when he made no moves to open his home to her, Natalia said, "I care about you and Holt, despite all that's happened, That's the only reason that I'm here. I never want you or Holt to be hurt."

"Hurting my wife hurt me."

Even though Jessie Belle was dead, Natalia's feelings toward her hadn't changed. "I'm not here to talk about Jessie Belle," she responded. "We are never going to agree when it comes to her. I just came to warn you about Reina."

He shook his head as if he pitied her.

Still, she continued, "For your safety, you need to distance yourself from her. Something's not quite right with her."

He gave her a bitter chuckle. "Coming from you, that's a laugh."

Natalia sighed. "I've warned you," she stated, thinking

that she'd done all that she could. "Whatever happens from this point forward is on you."

When she turned away, Traynor called after her, "Why did you do it?" he asked.

She turned back to face him.

He said, "What happened to your father was tragic, but do you believe he would have agreed with your actions? Do you think he'd be proud of what you did to my wife?"

Natalia thought about once again, telling Traynor that she had nothing to do with Jessie Belle's death. Instead though, she said, "We're going in circles and I don't want to do that." She paused. "Traynor, I don't care how you feel about me right now. The only thing I care about is warning you and letting you know that you need to focus on the real psychopath in your circle and that is Reina. Not me. She's the one you need to be concerned with or you'll be very sorry."

Then she turned and walked to her car, never looking back at Traynor.

****

Chrissy swallowed a pill and then drank water to wash the medication down. Since she had been on the meds, her mood swings did not occur as frequently. She was able to concentrate more—and she had to admit, she felt better physically and mentally.

The only thing was, more and more she condemned

herself for all of the bad choices she had made in the past. She blamed Sabrina. It was all her talk about God and second chances.

There are no second chances for people like me. That was what Chrissy told herself over and over.

"I'm not doing this today," she whispered. "I'm not going to beat up on myself for things that I can never change."

When she heard the lock in the front door click, she turned to the door. Sabrina was home.

Chrissy pushed her thoughts aside and pasted on a smile when Sabrina entered the apartment. "Hey, how was your day?"

"Great. How about yours?"

"I got a call from Food Lion. They want to interview me for a full-time position."

Sabrina put her purse down on the coffee table and when she looked up, she frowned. "What did you say?"

"I told them if they had something part-time, I was interested. I want to keep my job with the real estate office."

Sabrina blinked as if she were confused. "I thought you were thinking about getting your real estate license."

"I'm still thinking about it."

Sabrina studied her for a moment. "Something's bothering you, Chris. She paused, but Chrissy didn't say anything. Then, Sabrina added, "Don't worry, I'm not going to pry. I just want you to know that I'm here when you're ready to talk about whatever it is."

Chrissy nodded. "I know," she said with a smile. "Thank you for not being pushy. I appreciate it."

"What would you like for dinner?" Sabrina asked walking past her into the kitchen.

"I don't care." She shrugged. "Surprise me," she said as she walked toward her bedroom. Inside her own space, she could take her thoughts back to where she was before Sabrina came home. She could go back to her past where she could wallow in all of the bad decisions she'd made.

****

Traynor was in the midst of preparing for his sermon when he put his pen down. He stood and walked toward the steps that led to the attic. He felt led that that was where he was supposed to be.

Once up there, he sat down, wondering what this was all about.

What do you have to show me, Lord?

He felt the stirrings of anxiety in the pit of his stomach. Traynor wasn't sure that he was prepared for what he would find up there. However, he could not escape the feeling and the pulling.

He reached for the box that he'd held in his hands a few days ago and opened it. Right on top was Jessie Belle's journal from her sixteenth year, but he reached for another journal right under that one. He caressed it in his hands for a moment.

He hadn't been ready, but he was ready now to find

out more about his late wife.

Traynor opened the first journal his hands touched.

June 12, 1970

I met the most handsome man earlier today. Pastor Traynor Deveraux. The good Lord sent this good-looking man to preach the Gospel to the folk here in Mayville. Ma and Papa really like him and so do I.

If only he had come to sweep me off my feet and whisk me away to some place like Atlanta, Dallas or Los Angeles. I'm tired of living in this hick town. Since Brockton left, there isn't much left for me in Mayville.

Ma don't think I'll be able to find a good husband because I'm no longer pure (her word). She don't understand that Brockton and I loved each other. He wanted to marry me, but with him being white, he was scared to tell his parents that he loved a black girl. Guess he really wasn't man enough.

I loved him though and I tried to tell him that if we'd had our babies—there wasn't nothing his parents could do—we would be a family now and we'd be rich. Brockton is sure to play for the NFL because he's good. He even got a full scholarship to play football in college. He's gonna be the first boy from Mayville to play for the NFL.

Sad thing is that he chose to leave me behind. I blame Ma because she made me get rid of my babies. I was able to hide my last pregnancy until it was too late to have an abortion. Truth is I don't know just how pregnant I was, but enough for Ma to finally figure out my secret. I didn't get real big 'cause I was so small, I guess.

When Ma found out, she took me quick to see the midwife. I told her I wanted to keep my baby.

Ma didn't care though. She took me to see that midwife anyway. She told Ma that I'd have to have the baby the regular way. It was too soon and my baby died. My little girl went to heaven to be with the Lord. I never got to see her because I fainted from the pain.

The only thing I remember from that night is the pain. I never hurt so bad in my life. Seems like I woke up 'cause I heard my baby cry, but then I felt a sharp pain that almost squeezed the life outta me. That pain had such a hold on me that I could feel something gush out. Ma told me later that it was the afterbirth.

That night had me so mixed up because at times, I thought I heard my baby crying, but Ma said I didn't. She said the baby was born dead.

Every now and then, I have these dreams where I hear a baby crying. I see vague images of Ma holding a baby, but it can't be real 'cause I'm pushing. Panting hard, trying to bring a life I won't be allowed to raise. When I try to talk to Ma about it, she doesn't want to discuss what happened that night. Ma says it's better to just forget what happened.

How can I forget what I don't remember?

Traynor's hands were shaking when he closed the journal, unable to read anymore. What was this nonsense? Jessie Belle had been a virgin on the night they consummated their marriage. There was blood, so she couldn't have been pregnant before they met. None of this made sense to him.

Was she just writing about a fantasy? A fantasy concerning this boy, Brockton? Jessie Belle never discussed anyone she dated during her high school years. Traynor had just assumed that she had been very sheltered.

Two pregnancies.

She could not have been a virgin if she had been pregnant twice.

He stared down at the journal. Traynor did not want to read any more, but he needed answers to the questions that came from what he'd just read. He took a deep breath and flipped to another page. And then another and another until he found where she wrote about the day they were married.

June 23, 1970

I can hardly contain my joy! Today was my wedding day and I married the eloquent and handsome Traynor Deveraux. I am a First Lady just like Ma. The way Traynor looks at me—I know he loves me and I am going to be the best wife in the world to him.

I feel bad starting our marriage with a lie, but I don't want Traynor to think I'm a floozy. Ma made a tiny packet of blood for me to sprinkle in the bed tonight. We have to make him believe that he married a pure, innocent virgin. He's such a good man and I care what he thinks of me.

I can't wait to leave Mayville with him. He comes from a wealthy family and already owns his own house—our home. It sounds fabulous. Traynor and I are an attractive couple and together, our ministry will be as big as Billy Graham's—if not bigger. We will live like the rich and famous.

Traynor sat there re-reading that page over and over. He had no words.

He had been nothing but a blind, lovesick fool from the very beginning. Jessie Belle had manipulated him from the day they met. He felt a numbness spreading throughout his body as he wondered if she ever really loved him at all. He didn't know for sure since their whole life was built upon lies.

Traynor felt sick to his stomach.

Chapter 17

Dressed in black, Natalia waited with a pair of binoculars until dark before easing out of her car. She slipped on a pair of gloves before checking the fake rock near the steps to the porch and smiled.

She hadn't been sure, but there it was. Reina had hidden a key beneath that rock. Natalia could not believe that people continued to hide extra keys under something like this. It shouted 'key to my house found here' in her opinion.

Carefully, she put the key in the lock, then stepped inside.

Reina was out having dinner out with Frankie. Natalia knew because she had been following her all afternoon. Now, she had this opportunity to see what she could find out about Reina. She had to find something that she could take to the police or at least something that would convince Traynor that he needed to protect his family from her.

Natalia went from room to room until she found the master bedroom. This was most likely where she would find something. She knew that Reina would not keep her secrets out in the open.

Starting in the closet, she searched the shelves, then looked around the bedroom before she got on her knees and looked under the bed.

"Yesss," she whispered as she pulled out a box. Taking just a moment, she opened it and looked through the items. Inside was a birth certificate, passport, photos and newspaper articles. She didn't stop to look at any of those items closely. Digging deeper, she found a tattered journal at the bottom.

Natalia slipped it into her purse before putting the rest of the contents back inside.

She quickly pushed it back under the bed and rushed out of the room.

Natalia left the house, got into her car and drove away without one glance backward.

Her heart was still pumping fast when she returned home. She sat down on the sofa, waiting for the trembling to stop. Natalia could not believe she had actually broken into someone's home.

Natalia pulled the worn journal out of her purse and opened it. She was anxious to learn more about Reina Cannon and she hoped that there would be something inside this book that would give her the information she needed.

She muttered a curse. There was a birth certificate

and passport inside that box and if she'd been thinking, she would have taken those as well, or at least looked at them. She'd just been so focused on getting out of the house. Oh well, she was not about to go back over to Reina's house. This journal would have to be enough.

****

Her face clouded with uneasiness, Chrissy sat down on the edge of Sabrina's bed. "Does God really forgive all sins?" The question still weighed so heavily on her heart.

"Yes, He does," Sabrina said, having patience no matter how many times Chrissy asked that question. "He loves you so much and that's why He gave His only Son to die for our sins." She surveyed Chrissy's face a moment before asking, "Honey, what's going on with you?"

She looked away hastily, then moved restlessly. "I did something that was really terrible, Sabrina," she admitted aloud for the first time.

"We all can tell that story."

Chrissy shook her head. "What I did was really horrible." Tears rolled down her cheeks. "I was so angry, Sabrina. At the time, I didn't know that something was wrong with me."

Sabrina was instantly concerned. "Wrong with you? What do you mean? Are you sick?"

"Not in the way you think." She took a deep breath and said, "I have bipolar disorder. I found out when I was in Philly."

Sabrina looked relieved as she reached over and hugged her. "Honey, it's okay. They have medication for that."

"I know; I'm on medication and I've been seeing a therapist," she confessed. "I've been on meds for the past six months."

"Really? Why didn't you tell me?"

"I didn't tell you because I was ashamed."

"You have nothing to be embarrassed about," Sabrina assured her.

"You don't understand," Chrissy stated. "It's more than just my illness. It's what I've done."

"Just tell me," Sabrina urged softly. "You know you can tell me anything. And you may feel better talking about it."

Chrissy let a lot of moments pass. "It was me," she finally stated. When she tried to continue, her voice wavered. "I pushed Jessie Belle. I was there that night. I was the one who did it."

Sabrina gasped in shock. "Chrissy…."

"I was so angry with her," she spoke quickly.

"Tell me everything. How did that happen?"

Her hands, hidden from sight, twisted nervously in her lap. She took a deep breath as if she were about to begin a long story. "I came to Raleigh to see Jessie Belle earlier that day because I needed money. She taunted me and laughed. It made me crazy, Sabrina. I wanted to make her pay, so I went back to the house that evening and she was standing out on the balcony. She turned around and saw me and I don't know…I panicked and pushed her." She accepted a tissue from Sabrina and wiped the tears that gushed down her face.

"I know you really feel bad about it, Chrissy."

She sighed. "I didn't at first," she admitted, "but lately, I've been thinking a lot about her and I know that I never should have done that, Sabrina. It was wrong. I am no better than she was." Chrissy looked up. "Do you still think God will forgive me? I mean, this was horrible and…."

Sabrina smiled when she nodded. "He will. You have to repent and ask Him for forgiveness, and then, He will forgive you." She waited a moment and said, "If you'd like, we can pray together."

"You would do that with me?" she asked as if she were surprised. "Even after what I just told you?"

"Yes. Of course. If God will forgive you, who am I? Of course, I forgive you. And of course, I will pray with you." She took Chrissy's hands into hers, then bowed her head. "Repeat after me," Sabrina stated. "Dear Lord Jesus, I know I am a sinner, and I ask for Your forgiveness. I believe You died for my sins and rose from the dead. I trust and follow You as my Lord and Savior. Guide my life and help me to do Your will. In your name, Amen."

Chrissy repeated the words as instructed. She looked up and waited a moment before asking, "That's it?"

Sabrina nodded.

"So, I'm forgiven just like that?"

"Just like that." Sabrina smiled.

Chrissy let another moment pass. "Should I feel different? Because I don't."

Sabrina embraced her. "Chrissy, I know that sometimes it's difficult to feel forgiven, but that's because you don't know the great depth of God's love in the power of forgiveness that is found in the sacrifice of Christ. His infinite love is greater than your finite sin."

Chrissy looked up at her friend with an effort. "So what do I do now?"

"What do you want to do?" Sabrina asked.

"I just know that I don't want to go to jail." Chrissy began to sob. "I'm so s-sorry for what I d-did."

"We don't have to figure this out right now. Why don't you go lay down for a while and just rest? I'll be right here when you wake up. And then, we can figure it all out."

Chrissy nodded. But then, she said, "You're not going to tell anybody, are you?" She didn't think Sabrina would betray her, but Chrissy had to ask.

"No," Sabrina responded. "You can trust me. Chrissy, we will figure out what to do next together. You have my word. I won't abandon you."

Chrissy hugged Sabrina again, before she turned to her bedroom. All she wanted to do right now was rest.

****

As soon as Reina entered her house, she felt as if something was not quite right. Her shrewd eyes traveled the living room, searching to see if anything was out of place. Unable to ignore the strange feeling in the pit of her stomach, Reina went through all the rooms of her home before she headed to her bedroom.

Inside there, she walked straight to her bed, knelt down and removed the box from beneath it. Everything looked undisturbed, so she closed it and returned it under the bed. Yet, Reina could not escape the uneasiness she was feeling.

Maybe it was all that was going on in her life right now. What she needed to do was move up the final stages of her plan. She did not want to risk someone else interfering in her life.

Reina walked out of the house into her garage. She unlocked a cabinet and opened the doors. Inside one large leather tote was an ample supply of cash, including the fifty thousand that Mike had stolen from the church. The other tote included clothing, several copies of social security cards, birth certificates, driver's licenses, and other necessities. Intuition told her to put what she called her escape packages into the trunk of her car now.

She was probably being overly cautious, but Reina had lived on her instincts for so long…there was no point in changing now. She hoped that she wouldn't need anything in this tote, but if she did Reina would be ready.

She turned to go back into the house, but stopped in her tracks. Reina went back to the cabinet. She retrieved a gun.

If the threat she felt were indeed real, then Reina would definitely be prepared. She locked the door to the cabinet, turned off the light and returned to the house.

But even though she had taken precautions, the uneasy feeling she had would not disappear. Reina went from room to room but found nothing out of place.

It is just nerves, she told herself.

Then, something came to her mind and she rushed out the front door to the faux stone in her yard.

The key was there. But still....

She'd never considered an alarm system before, but with this feeling she had tonight, Reina decided it should be a priority.

The feeling was so strong that Reina placed the gun under her pillow right before going to bed. She had gone through the house three times, checking the windows and doors to make sure everything was locked.

But if anything should happen, she was prepared.

****

Today is the big day!

I'm going to formally introduce myself to my mother. I've waited such a long time for this, but timing was important.

She accepted my invitation to lunch finally. I booked a private room so that we would not be disturbed. This is a special occasion and I want our reunion to be perfect.

It's almost time so I'll write more when I get back.

I am so ANGRY now!

Everything was going fine until I told Jessie Belle Deveraux that she was my mother! She denied it vehemently, but I could see the truth in those gray eyes of hers. The fury that glimmered in her gaze reflected in my gray eyes as well. Gloria had told me how Jessie Belle cried the night I was born; how she begged her mother to let her see her daughter, but they told her that the baby was dead. I offered to take a DNA test to prove my claim, but she wasn't interested.

I knew she was selfish, but to turn her back on the child she once claimed to want. I have a brother that I want to get to know. I bet she thinks that her family would never understand, but that's not true. Traynor and Holt would be okay, I'm sure of it. I've never really met them, but I've heard nothing but good things about them.

Natalia sat on her sofa, the journal in her lap. Even though her mouth was wide open, she sat there until she had read Reina's private thoughts cover to cover.

The entries had her stunned.

I can't believe this, Natalia thought.

She wondered for a brief moment if someone would write a bunch of lies in a journal. Not that she doubted Reina was telling the truth—some of it was just hard to comprehend. Reina was Jessie Belle's daughter.

Reina's journal said that Jessie Belle didn't know about her, but once Reina went to her, she should have accepted it. It just proved what Natalia already knew – that Jessie Belle was selfish and self-absorbed.

Natalia's eyes widened. Traynor and Holt had no idea

of her relationship to them. She had to warn them. But how? I can't get Traynor to listen to anything I have to say. He won't believe me about this.

Then, Natalia had a thought. He would believe Mary Ellen. All she had to do was convince her that she was telling the truth about Reina. She would give the journal to Mary Ellen if necessary.

She hoped Reina had no idea that it was missing. She'd been very careful, but thinking back on her actions, it was a stupid move. What was she thinking to break into Reina's house? If she ever found out…

Natalia shuddered at the thought.

She tried to convince herself that Reina would never try to harm her—after all, Natalia didn't have anything that would tie Reina to Mike or Charlotte's deaths. All she had was this journal and this was only proof that she had deliberately set out to ingratiate herself with the Deveraux family. Still, Natalia truly believed that Reina had something to do with Mike and Charlotte's death and if she did, she was a psychopath. Traynor and Holt needed to know who they were dealing with.

Chapter 18

Reina had followed Jessie Belle to Raleigh with the hopes of getting to know her mother, but the woman never gave her the time of day. She had Holt and she seemed content with being a mother to just her son. Reina envied the life Holt had—the love of his parents and a life of privilege. She often wondered if he really understood just how lucky he was. She had been robbed of all of that, of loving parents, a real home and family.

Reina touched the tiny mole on her lip—just like the one Jessie Belle had, yet no one ever made the connection. She considered that her bluish gray eyes and honey blond hair color overshadowed that small imperfection.

She wondered whom she resembled in her biological family. Outside of her eyes and the mole, she didn't look like her mother. Jessie Belle had been quick to point that out, the day Reina announced she was her daughter.

"Thank you for meeting me," Reina stated as she stepped aside for Jessie Belle to enter the private room in the restaurant.

Instead of being impressed, Jessie Belle walked over to the table, sat down and asked, "Why did you want to meet with me?"

"There's something we need to discuss."

Jessie Belle sighed impatiently. "If you're going to blackmail me about the prostitutes, just do it. I'm not giving you a cent."

Reina shook her head. "You have this all wrong," Reina stated. "You were wronged a long time ago and I want to make things right."

She looked confused. "What are you talking about?"

Reina decided to get right to it. There was no need to stretch it out. "Jessie Belle, you were led to believe that your daughter died."

She gave her a narrowed glinting gaze. "Reina, I don't know what you're up to, but I never had a daughter. I only have one child and his name is Holt."

"I know that you were pregnant when you were sixteen," she interjected. "It was your second pregnancy."

Jessie Belle gasped, but recovered quickly. "Then you should know that I aborted those pregnancies."

"You aborted one, but had to go through the delivery on the second."

She was quiet, but for just a moment as if she was trying to figure all of this out. "How do you know all this?" she demanded.

Reina smiled. "Your mother had the midwife tell you that your daughter died, but she didn't...I didn't die." She paused, giving Jessie Belle time to absorb those words. "Gloria, the midwife, took me home and she raised me. She told me all about you before she died."

Uncertainly crept into her expression, as if one half of her believed Reina and the other half didn't. But what she said was, "I don't believe you."

"It's true," Reina insisted. "I'm your daughter." She stepped closer to her. "Just look at me." Reina was sure that when Jessie Belle looked at her, that would be all that it would take.

Jessie Belle studied her for a moment. "You don't look anything like me or Brockton."

Reina's breath caught in her throat. "But, but, I do. I have a mole on my lip just like you."

Jessie Belle shrugged. "So do a lot of other people," she uttered. Then with her eyes narrowed, she added, "I know all about people like you. You found out some information about me and now you're claiming to be my long lost daughter. Reina, you have been trying to be a part of my world since the day we met. It's just not going to happen, dear. Not even with this little lie that you've made up."

"I am telling you the truth," she insisted. "We can have a DNA test performed."

Jessie Belle continued to gaze at her. "Okay, let's say you're the child I gave birth to—what do you expect to happen?"

"You're my mother. We can make up for all the time that was stolen from us." She paused, then added, "Don't you want that?"

"Reina, I need you to listen to me. You will never be a part of my family. I'm sorry. I don't know what you've been through or what would make you say this, but I'm sorry."

"I am your family, Jessie Belle," she pleaded. "I'm your daughter."

She shook her head. "My husband would never understand. Besides, if what you're saying is true, there's no reason for us to do this connecting thing you're talking about. Your life didn't turn out bad."

Her words set Reina's heart on fire. "I can't believe you," she snapped in anger. "You really are a selfish witch. You have no idea what I went through—what hell your mother condemned me to—I needed you."

Without a hint of emotion, Jessie Belle said, "What you need is a therapist."

Jessie Belle's rejection had hurt deep. Her own mother wanted nothing to do with her—she had been discarded like a piece of trash...twice.

The next day, Jessie Belle was pushed over the balcony. When she heard about it, Reina had no feelings one way or the other regarding what happened to her mother. Instead, she decided to bide her time and take away from Jessie Belle what she valued most—her family.

Reina picked up the packet containing tickets for a cruise...for her family. She'd just purchased them and she planned to surprise Traynor and Holt with them later in the week. She'd convince them that this was just a gift since they'd been through so much. Then once they were on the cruise, she would tell them everything.

Traynor would understand why she waited to tell them, and he would welcome her into the family officially. Holt would be stunned of course, but in time, he would get used to the idea of having a big sister, especially since she'd already bonded with Frankie. She decided that a cruise was the perfect place for all of them to bond.

The thought brought a smile to her lips. Reina hoped they would be as excited as she was about the trip. They would be. Then, she would have what Jessie Belle was never willing to give her.

She would have her family.

****

Natalia greeted Mary Ellen when she arrived at the restaurant.

"I don't know why I agreed to meeting you," Mary Ellen said as she slid into the booth across from Natalia. "But I'm here, so say whatever you have to say."

Natalia didn't like Mary Ellen, but this was important. So she got straight to the point. "Reina is Jessie Belle's daughter," Natalia announced.

Mary Ellen glared at her. "What? Jessie Belle only has one child."

"That's what I thought too, until I read Reina's journal," Natalia stated. "Apparently, Jessie Belle gave birth to her when she was sixteen. She was told that the child had died, but the midwife took the baby home and raised her as her own."

Mary Ellen was silent for a moment as if she were considering Natalia's words. "This was in Reina's journal?"

"Yes."

"How did you end up with her journal?" she asked, her eyes narrow with skepticism.

"That's not a concern of yours," Natalia replied. "The only reason I came to you with this is because I can't seem to get through to Traynor. He won't listen to anything I tell him."

"Surely you can understand why," Mary Ellen responded. "But about this...I don't know why Reina would write lies in a journal, but Jessie Belle was a virgin when she married Traynor. She told me so."

Natalia gave her a slight chuckle. "You and I both know that Jessie Belle has been known to tell a lie or two."

Mary Ellen dismissed the comment with a slight wave of her hand. "I don't believe it, Natalia."

"Jessie Belle was not this sweet little angel you and Traynor want to believe she was. Did you know about the prostitutes?"

She frowned and shook her head like she was confused. "What are you talking about?"

"She ran a stable of girls. She was a madam, Mary Ellen."

"I don't believe you."

"We don't have time to argue about Jessie Belle right now. This is all about Reina and you need to find out what she wants with Traynor and Holt." Natalia pulled the tattered journal out of her purse. "You can read it for yourself and you'll see that Reina and Holt were not Jessie Belle's only children—they are the two surviving ones. She was pregnant before she had Reina."

Mary Ellen looked down at the journal. "If what you're saying is true, this is going to devastate Traynor," Mary Ellen said. She shook her head. "I can't do this to him."

"He deserves to know the truth," Natalia argued. "He's lived in deception far too long, don't you think? Plus, I don't trust Reina. How do we know that she's not going to cause Traynor and Holt some kind of harm."

Mary Ellen considered Natalia's words. "Don't you say anything to anybody," she stated. "I'll get in touch with you after I verify the validity of this journal."

"There's more," Natalia said. "Something that's not in that journal, but something that's important."

Mary Ellen said nothing, just waited.

"Reina was having an affair with Mike Jennings before he died. She was in Florida with him before Jessie Belle's funeral. What we don't know is whether he was alive when she left—I'm betting that he wasn't."

Mary Ellen's mouth opened wide, but not a word came out.

"One more thing…I wasn't the one who tried to kill

Jessie Belle. I'm betting that it was Reina. She confronted Jessie Belle and it didn't turn out the way she expected. She wrote about the meeting in her journal."

Now her eyes opened as wide as her mouth. "Do you know what you're saying?"

Natalia nodded. "The woman is a psychopath and her own words in that journal will prove it to you. She didn't exactly write this, but from what she said, I believe she killed the people who raised her. She did write about how she was sexually abused for years by the man she thought was her father. She got pregnant by him, but her son didn't survive. After her baby died, her mother told her the truth of her birth. They died in a fire a few days later. Like I said, she doesn't say that she killed them, but all you have to do is read her journal." She met Mary Ellen's stunned gaze. "I thought Jessie Belle was evil, but even with all of her lies and manipulations—her daughter is much worse. She could be a murderer, Mary Ellen."

"Natalia, even if Reina is claiming to be Jessie Belle's daughter—this journal really proves nothing."

"Maybe not, but a DNA test can," she responded. "What I know for sure is that Reina is not the person you all think she is. If you care anything about Traynor and Holt—tell them to stay away from her. Because if things don't go her way, there's no telling what she might do." She paused. "Just ask Mike and Charlotte and her parents."

****

Natalia hoped that Mary Ellen would be able to get through to Traynor. Those were her thoughts as she unlocked her front door. But then, she screamed when just before she stepped inside, she felt something pressed into her back.

"Hurry up. We don't want to draw any unnecessary attention," the voice behind her said. Natalia did as she was told. She waited until she was in her home and the front door was closed before she turned to face Reina. "What do you want?" she asked, and wondered if Reina had figured out that she was the one who stole her journal.

"Sit down over there," Reina ordered, pointing the gun she held toward the sofa. "We need to talk."

"We don't have anything to talk about," Natalia responded, eyeing the weapon in her hand.

Reina's eyes narrowed. "Oh there's a lot to discuss. Now move."

Natalia walked into the living room and slowly sat down on the sofa. Reina stood above her.

"You are such a nuisance," Reina said. "Why couldn't you just mind your own business?"

Although her heart was beating fast, Natalia did everything she could to keep her voice calm. "What are you talking about, Reina?"

"What did Charlotte tell you?"

She kept her face straight, hoping that she gave away nothing. "Just that you were in Florida with Mike,"

Natalia responded.

"Did she tell you that I was having an affair with him?"

Natalia just stared at her, said nothing. She didn't want to say anything that would upset Reina even more.

The blank look on her face must have given it away to Reina. She said, "She did tell you that. Well, you can't believe everything Charlotte says. She was a recovering drug addict. She probably saw blue cows, too."

Natalia glanced over at the door, then quickly turned back at Reina. "Doesn't it bother you that everyone close to you has ended up dead? I know if it were me, I'd feel some type of way."

Reina's eyes narrowed. "I'm not sure what you're implying."

It was the thought of all that Reina had done to her friends that made Natalia say, "I have proof that you were the one who was with Mike in that apartment."

"Oh really," Reina said calmly. "Where is this proof you're speaking of?"

"Somewhere safe."

Reina laughed. "You're bluffing."

"I'm not. You have a lot of secrets, Reina and I think you'll do anything to keep them hidden," Natalia stated. She tried to think of a way to convince Reina to put away the gun. "But if you leave right now, I won't say a word to anyone about…this visit."

Reina did not respond.

Then Natalia had another thought. Maybe if she got

Reina talking. Maybe she would lower her guard. Maybe then, she'd be able to escape. It was risky, she knew that. But what other choice did she have? Natalia said, "From the very beginning, you have reminded me of someone." She paused. " Jessie Belle Deveraux was your mother."

Reina was shocked, but recovered quickly. "I can't wait to hear how you came up with this theory of yours."

"My theory is simple," Natalia stated. She continued even though her heart was pounding. "Jessie Belle rejected you, which made you angry and then you pushed her over that balcony."

"Interesting theory, but no evidence …" Her eyes. Reina's eyes told a story of their own. Natalia could almost see the evilness within her and she was scared.

Natalia kept on anyway. "I don't need an admission from you," she told Reina. "I just want you to stop pointing that gun at me and leave my house. If you do that, I'll see that you get your journal back."

Reina regarded her quizzically for a moment. "What journal?"

Natalia did not respond. She had foolishly said too much.

A shadow of alarm touched Reina's face. "You broke into my house? Where is it?"

She could barely get the words out through all of the fear she felt. "I have it someplace safe," Natalia stated. "If you harm me in any way, it will be turned over to the authorities."

Reina took a step closer to Natalia, her eyes

conveying the fury within her. "I want my journal back."

"That's not going to happen." Natalia shook her head. "Not as long as you keep pointing that gun at me."

After a moment of thought, she tucked the gun into her waistband. "Where is my journal?" The gun was gone, but not her anger.

Taking a deep breath, Natalia stood up. "It's in my office." If she could just make it to her office and into the panic room, she could call the police.

"I'm going with you."

She had just taken a few steps when she felt a sharp prick on her arm. "What …" she said, looking down to where Reina had pierced her skin.

"I'm afraid I can't let you run around telling these little tales to other people."

The edges of darkness surrounded Natalie and she thought of all that was good in her life, especially Dean. Would she ever see him again?

As she felt her breathing becoming shallow, she prayed, Dear Lord, please don't let me die. Help me….

****

Reina slipped on a pair of gloves, and then searched through Natalia's office and then the rest of the house. The witch hid it well, she thought in frustration when she didn't find the journal.

She was not about to spend the rest of the day searching while an unconscious Natalia lay on the living room floor. Reina muttered a curse. She was going to have to get rid of another mess of someone else's making.

All Natalia had to do was mind her business, but from the moment they met, the twit kept interfering in her life. Now, she had to die.

Reina couldn't risk another drug overdose – that might surely, somehow lead to her. And no one would believe that Natalia would take her own life—she was too self-centered for that.

What was she going to do? She broke into a smile when she eyed the curling iron in Natalia's bedroom. Reina turned it on, and then knocked it to the floor near the curtains.

She pulled out a match and lit it, and watched as it floated to the floor.

She rushed out and quickly got into her rental car. She did not want to be anywhere near the Estates of Wakefield Plantation when the police and fire trucks arrived.

She lost her nervousness when she was back in her car. Reina was confident that now, her plans were back on track.

Chapter 19

Traynor opened the door and Reina stepped inside. "I'm sorry I'm late," she said. "I had a client and she didn't know what she wanted to do with her hair."

"Frankie and Holt are already here," he announced as he closed the door behind her. "We're all curious as to what this meeting is about."

She followed him into the living room.

Frankie greeted her with a hug. "Hey, lady."

"It's so good to see you," Reina murmured.

Holt embraced her next. "Good to see you."

She smiled with excitement. This was her brother that she held and soon, he would know it. She said, "I guess I shouldn't keep y'all waiting so I'm just going to say it. I booked a cruise for all of us."

Holt and Frankie looked at one another, then at Traynor, his surprise evident on his face.

Reina looked from one face to the other. She had expected a completely different reaction. "It's a seven day cruise for the entire family," she added, hoping that those words would make them more excited. "To the Caribbean in June."

Traynor was the first to break the stunned silence. "That's quite a generous gift, Reina."

"We appreciate this, but it's too much," Holt said. "Are you able to get your money back?"

This was not how this was supposed to go. "I don't want a refund. I want to go on this cruise with all of you. You've become my family—let me do this for you." Reina looked at Traynor. "Please."

When the doorbell rang, putting a halt to their conversation, Reina struggled to keep her composure. She had planned everything so carefully and now it looked as if everything was falling apart.

She had to convince them to come with her. She just had to.

****

Traynor returned to the living room with Mary Ellen in tow and the way her eyes widened showed that she was surprised to find Reina there. She had hoped to have this conversation with Traynor alone.

"Hello, Reina," she greeted.

"Mary Ellen," she responded coldly. Reina looked upset to see her.

"What brings you by?" Holt asked his godmother.

Reina's demeanor changed, and she didn't give Mary

Ellen a chance to respond. "We were having a family meeting and I don't appreciate your interrupting us."

Frankie's eyes rose in surprise to Reina's words, but she kept quiet.

Mary Ellen glanced over at Traynor and he seemed confused by Reina's comment as well. They don't know the truth yet.

"I came here to talk to Traynor. . . about you," she stated.

"About what?" Reina demanded, though her voice shook a little.

"The truth." Mary Ellen paused for a second. "It's time that everyone here knew the truth about you."

"I don't believe this," Reina muttered almost to herself. Here was another one interfering. Why couldn't Mary Ellen mind her own business? Things were about to go down a road Reina did not want to travel once again.

"What truth?" Traynor questioned, looking from Mary Ellen to Reina and then back to Mary Ellen.

There was silence for a moment until Mary Ellen said, "Reina claims to be Jesse Belle's daughter."

"WHAT?" Holt exclaimed. "My mother had no other children." He looked to his father for confirmation.

At first, Traynor's eyes widened. But then when he looked at his son, he lowered his head. A few seconds later, he returned his gaze to his son. "Son, there's a lot that you don't know about your mother."

Holt was already shaking his head before Traynor could even continue.

"I recently discovered that Jessie Belle was pregnant twice before we met," Traynor stated.

Holt and Frankie gasped.

Traynor was looking at Reina when he said, "Whether or not Reina is her daughter, only a DNA test can prove that."

"I'm more than happy to take one," Reina spoke up. The truth was finally in the open. "I had planned to tell you on the cruise." She smiled. Maybe it was better this way.

"There's more," Mary Ellen said, taking away Reina's smile. Her eyes were on Reina when she said, "Traynor, she's hurt people."

"What are you talking about?" Reina questioned. She kept her expression blank even though inside she was already shaking. "Who have I supposedly hurt?"

"Possibly Mike and Charlotte Jennings...your parents..."

"They weren't my parents," Reina shouted. "Gloria Ricks let her husband rape me over and over. They deserved to die for what they did," she cried.

"Reina, what are you saying?" Frankie asked, taking a step toward her.

"I'm saying they needed to pay for their sins and I made sure that they did."

"Dear Lord..." Traynor muttered.

Reina's eyes filled with tears. "Before Gloria died, I made her tell me about my real mother. She told me how badly Jessie Belle wanted me, but her mother told her that

I was dead. I was premature, but my will to live was strong—I always believed it was because of my mother's love for me."

"You wanted your mother to accept you," Mary Ellen said gently, "and when she didn't, you were determined to be a part of her family regardless."

She nodded as she wiped away her tears. "You understand?"

Mary Ellen nodded. "I do, but I don't understand why you hurt Mike and his wife. They didn't have anything to do with this."

"I wanted Traynor to come back to Raleigh, so I told Mike that I'd run away with him, but he had to resign. I didn't intend to stay with him, though. I just wanted to be with my family." Her tear bright eyes traveled from face to face. "I wasn't going to let anyone get in the way of our reunion."

Reina turned to look at Mary Ellen. "How did you find out all of this?"

"I don't think it really matters."

"You talked to Natalia," she said. "She stole my journal and that's how you found out."

Mary Ellen did not confirm or deny.

"Reina," Holt began. "I've always wanted a sibling."

"So did I," she said, her tears still falling. Her heart warmed at his words, but she still felt the chill of distrust. "All I've ever wanted is a family, but I'm not sure I'll ever have one." Reina reached into her purse and pulled out a gun.

"What are you doing with that?" Traynor asked as he stepped in front of Holt and Frankie.

"This is Natalia's fault," she told him as she waved the gun. "None of this would have to happen if she'd just minded her own business." Reina took a few steps back. "I know what you're all doing," she hissed. "You're trying to trick me."

"No, we're not," Holt said.

But her instincts told her that they were just being nice until they could turn her in. "Take out your cell phones and toss them over here."

"We just want to help you," Frankie said. "This is not who you really are, Reina."

She laughed. "You think you know me, but you have no idea. I am not some fool that you can just lock away for the rest of my life. I don't want to hurt you, so just do as you're told."

They exchanged glances, then the four of them all did as instructed. When she had dumped all of their phones into her tote, she said, "Traynor, I'm sorry it's come to this. This is not what I had in mind."

"Then let me help you, Reina."

When he took a step toward her, she held up the gun and he stopped. She shook her head. "I can't. I am not going to prison, Traynor. When I leave here, none of you will ever see or hear from me again. As long as you don't try to find me." More tears welled up in her eyes. "I love you, Holt. I love all of you, but not enough to let you lock me up."

Reina tossed the tickets onto the table. "Enjoy the cruise."

Traynor looked as if he wanted to move closer, but once again she trained her gun on him. "Don't do it," she warned.

His eyes never left Reina's. "You won't hurt me. This is not the woman I've come to know."

"I don't want to hurt you, but I won't let you get in my way, Traynor. I just want you to know that I don't blame you," Reina assured him. "Jessie Belle was the one who rejected me."

"Did you p-push her that night?"

"No," she replied softly. "She was never really nice to me, but she was still my mother even if she did reject me."

"I won't do that to you," Traynor assured her. "I would never reject you. I will be here for you, Reina."

"I really would love to believe that, but I can't. You want to have me locked up—to pay for my sins. I'm not about to let that happen, Traynor." She paused. "Natalia didn't learn her lesson, but I hope you will."

"What did you do to Natalia?" Mary Ellen asked with fear in her voice.

Reina must have realized that she'd said too much because of the look she gave Mary Ellen. "Don't try to find me," she said before rushing out of the room and through the front door.

Holt ran toward the door while Frankie quickly grabbed the house phone, dialing 9-1-1.

Mary Ellen released a sigh of relief.

Traynor dropped down to the sofa and sat in stunned silence.

"She's gone," Holt reported when he returned.

"I've called the police," Frankie announced. "They're sending a car to Natalia's house and one here."

Chapter 21

Chrissy spent most of the day reading the Bible. Pastor Poole had talked about David, a man after God's own heart. His words struck a chord within her, provoking her to read more about him.

David's deeds, which included murder, displeased the Lord, but God forgave Him. He was forgiven, but David suffered the consequences of his actions. Even though he committed an appalling sin, God still loved him.

Chrissy couldn't believe that and she brushed a tear from her cheek.

She was vaguely aware of Sabrina walking into the living room and taking a seat on the sofa.

Chrissy looked up, her cheeks tear-stained, while further tears gathered in the corners of her eyes. She closed her eyes as the next batch fell, spilling against the already damp pages of her Bible.

Without saying a word, Sabrina got up and handed her a tissue.

Chrissy patted the pages before dabbing at her eyes

and face. "I've made a decision," her voice quaked. "I need a favor from you."

"What do you need me to do?" she asked, stroking Chrissy's hair.

Tears fell freely as she responded, "I want you to come with me to Pastor Deveraux's house. It's time for me to come clean about what I did and accept the consequences."

"Are you sure about this, Chris?" Sabrina asked.

Through watery eyes, she stared at her friend and nodded. "God has given me peace with my decision. I know that He will be with me regardless of what happens. It's just a little overwhelming to acknowledge that I hurt someone—that I killed her."

Sabrina started to protest, but Chrissy stopped her. "She died as a result of the injuries sustained when I pushed her." She rocked in the chair she was sitting in. "For years, I wouldn't let myself believe that I'd actually done something like that. I made myself believe that Jessie Belle deserved what happened to her, but it was not my right. Her life was not mine to take."

Now, Sabrina had tears running down her face. "I'm so proud of you."

She stood up. "I want you to know how much I appreciate you. We have been through it, but we made it out. I used to think that I didn't have family, but I was wrong. You have been closer than any sister I could have. I love you."

The two women embraced. "I love you, too, girl."

After Chrissy went into her bedroom to grab her purse, Sabrina grabbed her keys and her bag. "Ready?"

Chrissy nodded. "I'm ready."

"Let's have prayer before we go," Sabrina suggested.

They bowed their heads and Sabrina prayed. "Amen," she murmured when they finished. Chrissy was not sure how this situation would turn out, but she was prepared to pay for her crime.

****

The police had been gone for almost fifteen minutes when Frankie and Mary Ellen returned to the living room with glasses of iced tea.

"I have a sister," Holt uttered, as if he couldn't believe it. "All this time, Reina knew and never said anything. But at least now we know why she kept inserting herself into our lives and we embraced her." He accepted the drink from his wife. "Thanks, babe."

"We treated her like a member of the family," Frankie said. "It's what she wanted—to be a part of our lives."

Mary Ellen offered Traynor a glass, but he refused it. She sat it down on the end table closest to his chair.

"All she had to do was tell the truth from the very beginning. We never would've turned her away," Holt stated.

"How do we really know that she's telling the truth?" Frankie asked. "It's pretty obvious that she's a very good liar."

"She's not lying," Traynor said, his voice sounding like he was still in shock. "I went through Jessie Belle's journals a couple of weeks ago, and they confirm that she was pregnant twice before we ever married," he said. "She was in love with a white football player at the high school."

Holt's eyes grew wide in his surprise. "She told me that she was a virgin on her wedding night. She said you were the only man she had been with—she was always telling me the importance of abstaining until marriage."

"Apparently, your mother lied to us both. She went to great extremes to prove that she was untouched." Traynor shook his head sadly. "I'm tired of all of the lies. I just wish that my love had been enough for her. I wish she would have trusted me."

"She loved you," Mary Ellen stated. "Never doubt that. She didn't want to tarnish the image you had of her."

"I placed her on a pedestal."

Mary Ellen agreed.

"Do you think we'll hear from Reina again?" Frankie inquired, her arms resting on her protruding belly.

"I don't think so," Traynor responded. "She wanted her mother most of all and Jessie Belle is gone. She was willing to do anything, even commit murder for the woman who gave birth to her, but it was all for nothing. Jessie Belle would have never accepted Reina."

The doorbell sounded.

"Who can that be now?" Holt questioned. "I hope

it's not the police coming back. I just want this day to end."

Frankie opened the door.

"Hi, my name is Sabrina and this is Chrissy. We would like to speak with Pastor Deveraux, if possible."

"Dad, you have some visitors," Frankie announced.

Traynor stepped into the foyer. "What can I do for you?" He tried to place them, but could not. "I'm sorry…do I know you?"

"No," they said in unison.

"Can we speak with you privately?" Sabrina asked.

"Sure. We can talk in my office." Inside there, he offered them each a seat, but Chrissy preferred to stand.

She spoke up first, wanting to get this over with. "The reason we came to see you is because I need to tell you something. I've given my life to the Lord, and now I can't go one more day without making this right."

Traynor wore his confusion on his face. "I'm afraid I don't understand."

"Pastor, I'm just going to get right to this. It started because Sabrina and I were prostitutes and we worked for your wife." She paused, expecting him to be surprised, but he kept his face blank, though he seemed to be studying her.

His eyes traveled over Chrissy's face, the smooth tawny complexion, the warm brown hair color. In just seconds, he rolled the thoughts over in his mind, did a few calculations and it was all clear to him; he knew why she looked so familiar.

"I didn't have a great relationship with Jessie Belle, but I did work for her."

He forced his attention back to her words. "I was told that my wife was never involved with prostitution. One of the girls who supposedly worked for her denied the claim."

"That was me and I lied," Chrissy said. "I lied to protect her—something she never did for me."

He nodded as he heard the bitterness in her voice. "Why are you here now?" Traynor asked, wondering if her words would put all of the pieces of the puzzle together. "What is it you want? Money?" he asked, though he suspected that this wasn't about money at all.

"No, Pastor." Chrissy glanced over at Sabrina. When her friend nodded, she turned back to him. "I came to make a confession."

"What is it?" he asked.

She took a deep breath and tears came to her eyes. She pushed the words out, "I was the one who pushed Jessie Belle over that balcony. We'd had words earlier that day…" Her voice died and she was quiet for a moment, but then, she continued, "There is no excuse for what I did. I sincerely regret my actions."

It was so quiet in the office as Traynor sat behind his desk, looking up at Chrissy, still studying her. He stayed thoughtful for a few more seconds that felt like hours. "You were the one who was attacked in Florida, weren't you?" he finally asked.

She nodded.

"Did Jessie Belle have something to do with your attack?" Traynor wanted to know.

She glanced at Sabrina. "Indirectly," Chrissy answered. "But that was no reason and I am so sorry, Pastor."

He observed her for another moment before asking, "But that's not the only reason you pushed her, is it?"

At first, Chrissy just looked at him and in his eyes, she could tell that he knew the whole truth. Her bottom lip quivered, but still, she said nothing.

Traynor said, "You know, don't you?"

"Know what?" Sabrina asked with a frown as she looked from one to the other.

But Traynor didn't take his eyes off of Chrissy. "Do you wear contacts?" Traynor inquired.

She nodded.

"What color are your eyes?"

Chrissy chewed on her bottom lip before responding. "Gray. Kids used to tease me about my eyes so I started wearing contacts."

Sabrina gasped and now she studied Chrissy. Softly, she said, "Jessie Belle is your mother."

After a moment and a sigh, Chrissy said, "She gave birth to me, but she was never a mother to me—not that she wanted to be."

"How did you know?" Sabrina asked. "How did you find out?"

Chrissy shrugged. "I could see a resemblance between us right away. Then when you mentioned she was from

Georgia, I thought we might be related, but I didn't expect that she was my birth mother. I wanted to know, though, so when she came to the hotel suite to talk to us, she used your hairbrush, do you remember?"

Sabrina half shook her head and half nodded. It had been a long time, too long for her to remember exactly.

"Anyway, I took some of the strands of her hair and had it tested with mine," Chrissy stated. "I found out a few weeks later, but I kept it to myself. It was a while before I said anything to her."

Chrissy sighed. The memory of that day formed in her mind.

"I have the DNA results," she told Jessie Belle. "As much as it sickens me to say this—you are my mother."

Jessie Belle laughed. "You're not the first to come here with that little scam. I only have one child."

"DNA doesn't lie."

"They can be faked, however," Jessie Belle uttered. "Since I wouldn't give you the money you asked for, you decided to come back and try this? Well, it won't work."

Chrissy removed her contacts. "Are you still going to try and deny me?"

Jessie Belle wasn't fazed. "You are not my daughter. I would never call a common whore a daughter of mine."

Chrissy's eyes watered, but she refused to let Jessie Belle see her cry. She would not give her the satisfaction of seeing the pain she caused by her words.

"You are no prize as a mother either."

"You told her and she denied it," Traynor stated

through her memories.

Chrissy nodded. "She made it clear that she would never have a whore for a daughter." Her eyes watered now like that had on that day when she'd gone to Jessie Belle and she blinked rapidly. "I couldn't before, but now I can finally forgive Jessie Belle."

"It's the right thing," Traynor said. "I've been walking around with my heart filled with unforgiveness and a thirst for revenge. But recent events have given me a clear view of the road that awaits me if I continue to travel this path."

Confusion crossed Chrissy's face. "I'm not sure what you're saying."

"Closing the door on bitterness is directed at restoring a peaceful and contented Christian walk. This has nothing to do with excusing or ignoring any embittering sinful actions of others, but it has everything to do with forgiving and not letting one's soul be controlled and tormented by the actions of another. Jessie Belle's actions affected all of us, but we cannot continue to let her torment our souls. I forgive her and I forgive you, Chrissy."

She blinked as if she didn't understand his words. "You're just going to let me walk out of here? You're not going to call the police?"

He shook his head. "My wife…your mother is dead. You have another chance to do some good and I hope you will take this opportunity to do just that."

She released a long sigh of relief. "I repented and

asked the Lord's forgiveness," Chrissy stated. "But I never thought that I'd have yours. I am so grateful for your forgiveness as well."

He smiled.

"I want to live the life the Lord has for me, Pastor."

"Thank you, Chrissy," Traynor said and his smile widened. "I needed this today of all days."

She glanced over at Sabrina before looking back at him. How could this news, what she'd told him make him smile? How could this be what he needed. "I'm not sure I understand."

"You have renewed my hope in humanity."

She nodded, then said, "Pastor, may I ask you something?"

"Sure and please call me Traynor."

"How did you know about me? Did Jessie Belle tell you?"

He shook his head. "She never mentioned having other children. But I found out recently about the events on the night you were born. She was drugged and confused...and young. She'd been told that you were stillborn, but she wrote in her journal that she heard a baby crying." He paused a moment before continuing, "I hope I am not offending you by saying that you look a lot like your mother."

"I had a DNA test done if you'd like to see just to be sure."

"I don't need those," he said. "I'm sure." Then after another moment, he asked, "If you don't mind my asking, who raised you?"

"I grew up in a group home. I was told that a woman named Gloria Richards or Ricks—I don't really know the last name, took me to a hospital in Georgia. She told a nurse that I had been abandoned by my mother and she left me there."

"When were you born?"

Chrissy frowned a little at all of his questions. But after the grace the he was giving to her, she was going to answer every one. "February, 1968."

He nodded and his eyes became brighter as if he had new understanding. "The reason I'm asking you all this is because it hadn't occurred to me until you came here...I think you may have a twin."

"Oh, my," Sabrina said.

Chrissy frowned. "What? A twin? Why do you say that?"

"Jessie Belle once told me that twins ran in her family. Her father was a twin...and she wrote in her journal about that night. How she was sure that she'd seen a baby, but she felt like she was still giving birth. When I first read the entry, I thought she'd just been hallucinating. But now I'm beginning to believe you are a twin. There was another woman who was here today...." Traynor went on to tell them about Reina's visit and her revelation.

"So you believe her?" Chrissy asked when he was finished. "You believe that she's my sister?"

"She believes it and also confronted Jessie Belle.

Reina was willing to take a DNA test for us to prove her claim."

"Wait, Reina?"

He nodded. "Reina Cannon. Do you know her?'

Chrissy looked at Sabrina once again and her friend's eyes were wide with the same surprise she felt.

"I don't really know her, but...." She didn't feel the need to explain that all to Traynor.

"Well anyway, you asked if I believe her and I do. Not only was she willing to take a DNA test, but she went through great lengths to be with my family. But what I found out is that Reina was raised by a Gloria Ricks, so I can only surmise that Gloria was only willing or maybe only able to keep one of you."

Chrissy was silent for a moment. "This is too much," she muttered. "I have a twin sister who is crazy. Being related to Jessie Belle was bad enough." She stopped short, then gave Traynor a short glance. "I'm sorry, Pastor...uh, Traynor."

He half-smiled. "Well, maybe we can begin to make some of this up to you." He stood. "Would you like to meet the rest of your family?"

To his surprise, Chrissy shook her head. "From what you just told me, they've been through enough. I don't want to complicate things further."

"You're not a complication. You're my son's sister."

That sounded so strange to her. "It's too soon," Chrissy said.

"I understand."

"And if I can ask one more favor," she began. "I would appreciate it if you not tell them about me." When the ends of his lips turned down, she added, "At least not right now."

He nodded as if he understood her decision. "You are a part of this family, Chrissy. We are here whenever you are ready to come home."

Those words made her feel better than she'd felt in a long, long time.

****

"There was a fire at Natalia's house," Mary Ellen announced after he'd let Chrissy and Sabrina out and then joined his family in the living room.

Before the women left, he'd filled them in on the rest of the story. How Natalia had also helped and how he prayed that she was all right. Now to hear this.

"Is she all right?" Traynor inquired.

Mary Ellen nodded. "She was taken to the hospital, but she's going to be okay."

"So…Reina?" he asked.

She nodded again. "It looks that way. It looks like she set the fire."

"Wow."

"None of us knew how sick Reina was," Holt stated. Now, he shook his head. "She seemed to really have it all together. She had me fooled."

"Reina fooled all of us," Frankie uttered. "I never

realized just how dark love could be, all kinds of love—she did all of this because she wanted her mother."

"Like Jessie Belle, Reina was motivated by love," Traynor interjected.

"But mom never would have killed anyone," Holt said. "She and Reina are nothing alike," he said, his voice strong as he defended his mother.

"Son, they are more alike than you know" Traynor said with a sigh. "After reading Jessie Belle's journal, I'm not sure I knew her at all."

"Those journals need to be destroyed," Frankie said. "Keeping it is only a sad reminder of Jessie Belle."

Holt agreed. "Get rid of them, Dad. All of them."

"I don't know," Traynor said after a moment. "It might be best to keep them for a little while longer."

They sat quiet for a moment before Holt changed the subject. "Who were the two women that came to see you?" he asked. "I've never seen them at church."

Traynor was quiet for a moment as if he were recalling every word of Chrissy's conversation. "That's a story for another night," he responded. Then it was his turn to change the subject. "Tomorrow, I'm going to visit Natalia. I owe that young woman a huge apology. She had nothing to do with what happened to Jessie Belle."

They talked for a few more hours, before Frankie, Holt and Mary Ellen left, all of them emotionally exhausted from their day. When he was alone, Traynor went up to the attic, then returned to the living room with one of Jessie Belle's journals in his hand. No matter what

Holt and Frankie said, there was no way he was going to get rid of any of the journals. One day, Chrissy might want to read it—she would need to read it to know that her mother really did love her.

Thinking about Jessie Belle, he wondered how he never really knew her. He remembered their last day together.

"I'm not getting any better, Traynor. I can feel it." Jessie Belle was seated in her wheelchair near the fireplace.

His eyes traveled to her gaze and he smiled. "Where is your faith?" Traynor noted that his wife was getting weaker, but he refused to lose heart—to lose faith. Especially since even in her weakened state, Jessie Belle wanted to attend church.

"I'm going to rest up this week, so that I won't miss church on Sunday." She paused a moment, and then said, "Traynor, I've put you through a lot, and I want you to know that I'm sorry."

"We don't need to go through all of this again," he told her. "We're not living in the past."

"Honey, indulge me."

"I love you, Jessie Belle."

She smiled. "I love you, too. I can't put into words, just how much, Traynor."

He nodded. "So, what is it you want to tell me?" he asked.

She spoke quickly, as if she had her words ready. "God has been so good to me. He brought me you and

Holt. I don't deserve either one of you, but He still blessed me."

"I can say the same thing," Traynor stated. "None of us can ever be deserving enough of God's many blessings."

"He gave me so many chances..." she said. "You know, every time I hear David's story, I feel encouraged. I just wish I'd taken all of the opportunities God gave me."

Traynor kissed her cheek. "You'll have other opportunities. Your life is not over, sweetheart."

She paused for a moment. "No, it's not," she murmured. "I have a lot of regrets, though. Some you know about and some you don't. There are things I wish I could go back and redo, but I can't."

"I think we all feel that way at one time or another," Traynor responded.

"I've hurt so many people including my own. What kind of person does that to her own?"

Traynor now realized that she was not just referring to Holt, but also her daughters. He had no idea if Jessie Belle ever realized that she had given birth to twins that night in February. In the end, they had mattered to her, but the damage was already done.

He prayed that the cycle of lies in Jessie Belle's family would finally be broken, and there would be no more secrets. Traynor had no idea what would happen to Reina and that made him sad. She was sick and she needed help before she destroyed herself.

At least there was hope for Chrissy. He prayed God would continue to give her the strength to deal with the consequences of her actions—she would have to live with Jessie Belle's blood on her hands for the rest of her life.

****

Natalia was thankful to be alive.

She remembered opening her eyes to thick smoke all around her and it had taken her a moment to realize that she was in her own house. She had tried to move, but her body felt heavy.

Fear had overtaken her as the truth sank in. The house was on fire. "Lord, please help me," she had pleaded repeatedly.

Natalia finally managed to drag her body to the window nearby, as she struggled to breathe. She could almost feel the heat of the fire on her back. Breathing became harder as she struggled to open the window. She knew that if she did not get some oxygen, she would pass out.

Finally, she heard the fire engine sirens. As they pulled up, Natalia's body seemed to shut down. She lost her vision and felt as if she was asphyxiating. Just when she thought she would pass out, she felt someone pick her up.

"You're going to okay," he told her.

As soon as Natalia was placed into the ambulance, her house exploded, splitting in two. She must have fainted because that was her last memory before waking up in the hospital.

"How long have I been here?" she asked the nurse who had just walked into her room.

"About two hours," she responded. "How are you feeling?"

Her head hurt and she felt a little nauseous. "Grateful," Natalia replied, her voice hoarse. "I'm thankful to be alive."

The nurse nodded as she checked her vitals.

"I'd like to take a shower."

"Sure. I'll get you a clean gown."

Her legs felt weak as she made her way to the bathroom. But inside the small space, she could see in the mirror that the smoke had darkened her hair and skin. As soon as she stepped into the shower and turned the water on, Natalie broke into sobs.

Even after her shower, Natalia still felt dirty. She could still smell the smoke, even in her freshly washed hair. She returned to the hospital bed and climbed inside with tears still rolling down her face.

Reina hated her enough to want her dead, but that alone wasn't the reason for Natalia's tears. Shame filled Natalia to the core. She was no better than the woman who had tried to kill her. Like Reina, she allowed bitter roots to defile her from the inside out. Natalia thought of the many times, she had wished death upon Jessie Belle.

God please forgive me.

"Natalia..."

She opened her eyes to see Dean standing in the doorway. "Come in," she urged, wiping away her tears.

"I just heard about what happened on the news. I'm glad you're okay." He kissed her.

"I can't get all this stuff off my skin," she whispered.

"I don't care. You're alive. That's all that matters to me," he told her.

Natalie's eyes teared up even more. "I thought I was going to die. Dean, I've never been so scared."

"You're safe, sweetie," Dean stated. "Natalia, I promise that you will never have to go through anything like this again. I will protect you."

"I was so afraid that I wouldn't have the chance to love you," she blurted. "You have been in my every waking thought since the day we met."

He smiled. "I had the same fear when I heard about the fire."

Natalia grabbed his hand and kissed it. "I'm glad that you're here. I feel safe now."

"I'm glad."

She looked into eyes that made her heart beat faster, simply because of the way he looked at her.

It was the way he looked at her that made her say, "Dean, there's something I need to tell you. I don't want any secrets between us. Once I tell you this, you may not want to be with me, but I need to be honest with you."

He shook his head, and his words assured her. "Believe me, there is nothing you can say or do to change the way I feel about you."

"There was a woman named Jessie Belle Deveraux …"

When she finished, Dean sat on the edge of the bed. Slowly, he ran his hand along her cheek, then traced her lips with a gentle finger. He leaned toward her and kissed her softly.

"You have been through a lot, but that's all over, sweetheart. The only way you can heal is through forgiveness."

"I've tried," Natalia admitted. "I've even prayed and asked God to help me forgive so that I can move past this, but then anger sets in and I can't."

"I think that may be because you've felt alone, but I'm here now," he told her. "You aren't by yourself anymore, sweetheart."

Natalia looked at the clock on the wall. "You should be on your way to Bible Study."

"I really don't want to leave you."

"I'll be fine, Dean. They're keeping me in the hospital tonight."

"I'll book a room for you at a hotel for when you get out tomorrow."

"You don't have to do that," Natalia said. "I'll be fine."

"We'll discuss this later," he responded. "I have to be in court tomorrow, but I'll be here as soon as I can."

"Okay."

He kissed her. "I thank God for you."

Natalia smiled. "Same here."

Chapter 22

Reina walked briskly into the Raleigh-Durham Airport. When she left Traynor's house, she stopped long enough to slip on a dark wig, a pair of brown contacts, and change her clothes. She discarded the gun in a dumpster and wired the money to three separate bank accounts.

"I need a ticket to Cancun," she told the airline representative. Reina chose Cancun because they had a flight leaving within the hour.

"When are you planning to return?"

"I'm actually planning to fly to New York from there."

It only took a few minutes for her ticket to be completed. She made it through the security checkpoint without a problem, but Reina didn't expect otherwise.

Soon she would be on a plane and far away from Raleigh.

When she arrived in Cancun seven hours later, Reina rented a car and drove forty miles to Playa del Carmen. The village was crowded with locals displaying their wares for sale, varying brightly colored jewelry, Mexican pottery and intricately woven baskets.

But though a festive air surrounded her, she fumed in silence over all that transpired in the last day. Traynor and Holt pretended they wanted to help her, but she didn't believe them—they were going to send her to jail. After all she'd been through, after all the plans she made, it was beyond disappointing.

Reina gritted her teeth as she seethed. Well, that plan didn't work, but she would stay in Playa del Carmen for a few days to relax and gather her thoughts.

She checked into her hotel and went straight up to her room. As soon as she settled down, Reina turned on her computer to check for news updates in Raleigh. From the app for one of the local Raleigh stations, she heard that police were looking for her; she was wanted for questioning, the broadcaster announced.

Reina groaned in protest when she heard that Natalia survived the fire. At least my journal is gone, she thought. There was nothing really incriminating in it, but it could still be damaging. She wasn't worried because it had been destroyed with Natalia's house. This will teach that witch to mind her own business.

An hour later, Reina ventured down to the bar across the street, choosing a spot in a darkened corner of the room. She ordered a Pina Colada, then sat back and took in the sights.

Soccer paraphernalia was everywhere as tourists and locals shared in the excitement of the game on the television. Outside, hordes of children were playing with a soccer ball on a side street.

The bar erupted in boisterous cheers and applause.

El Futbol.

Reina smiled. She was not much of a sports fan, so it did not matter who was winning. In fact, the only reason she was watching the game was that it was the only thing the bar had playing on television.

After her drink, she left the restaurant, but by the time she returned to her room, Reina felt the beginnings of a headache and attributed it to drinking on an empty stomach.

She crawled into bed and closed her eyes, hoping to ease the throbbing in her forehead. Reina had not had a migraine in years, but she felt as if one was coming on.

It was probably because of everything she had experienced in the past couple of days. Reina had no patience for mistakes. She had worked too hard on her plan and it was flawless, although she unfortunately had to make some adjustments, one being Charlotte and then Natalia.

She was furious about that.

Reina had not counted on Natalia going to Mary Ellen or the fact that anyone would take Natalia's accusations seriously. But Natalia was the sole reason why this hadn't worked out for her. Reina just hoped that one day, Natalia would have to pay.

****

The next day, Natalia was more than ready to leave the hospital. She had no home to go to, but a part of her was afraid that Reina would be waiting for her wherever she went.

Dean offered to put her up in a hotel, but she declined. Natalia did not want to sully his reputation in any way.

Police detectives visited her last night, questioning her about Reina. She told them as much as she knew. However, she was stunned to find that Reina's name was not really Reina Cannon. It was an alias.

"Hey cousin," Sabrina greeted from the doorway, interrupting her thoughts.

"What are you doing here?" She had never been so glad to see anyone. Natalia was still trying to figure out her next move.

Sabrina entered the room. "I came to take you home...actually, I'm going to take you back to my place. It's small, but clean and we have an extra bedroom."

Natalia almost sagged with relief. "Thank you, Sabrina."

"I'm so glad that you're okay."

"Me, too."

Sabrina sat down beside her on the bed. "I heard that Reina is still at large."

Natalia nodded. "I heard that, too."

"I think what you did was pretty admirable. Pastor Deveraux told me how you tried to warn them about her."

She sighed in resignation. "He has it out for me, Sabrina. He's been trying to prove that I attacked his wife. It wasn't me, but Traynor won't believe me."

Before Sabrina could tell her that she was wrong, they heard, "I do now," from the doorway.

Both Natalia and Sabrina looked up.

"I came to apologize to you, Natalia," Traynor said as he walked into the room.

She was stunned to see Traynor. Her face burned as she remembered all of the terrible things she'd said to him about Jessie Belle. "I need to apologize to you as well," she responded. "I was wrong to taunt you with all that your wife did. Instead of seeing the good in her...I focused on all the terrible things."

"I focused on all the good and was blind to the bad," Traynor admitted. "I have had to face the harsh reality of her actions. It's been painful, but it's time I see the person she really was."

Natalia nodded and asked, "Do you think Reina. . . whoever she really is. . . do you think she's gone?"

"I do," Traynor answered. "The detectives want to talk to her regarding the fire, Mike and Charlotte...I don't think she'll ever look back now that she's on the run."

"I don't know what I was thinking," Natalia uttered. "I had my suspicions about her, but I didn't think she would try to kill me. Charlotte tried to warn me, but I really didn't want to believe that she was a cold-hearted killer."

"Don't feel bad," Traynor said. "I never thought she was capable of everything she's done. What has come out of all this for me is that I'm a terrible judge of character."

"You just want to believe the best in people," Sabrina stated. "My mama once said that people will eventually show you who they truly are—you just have to accept the truth when they do."

Natalia and Traynor both nodded at those words of wisdom.

****

"God is not only the God of second chances; He is the God of another chance," Pastor Poolee said as he stood in the pulpit. "This is good news because most of us mess up the second chance fairly quickly. One of the amazing facets of God's character is His incredible patience with us. I believe Psalm 86:15 says it well: But you, O Lord, are a God merciful and gracious, slow to anger and abounding in steadfast love and faithfulness."

Chrissy turned to the scripture he referenced so that she could write it down.

"Micah 7:18 says, who is a God like you, pardoning iniquity and passing over transgression for the remnant of his inheritance? He does not retain his anger forever, because he delights in steadfast love. The Bible is full of people who received second chances, and even third and fourth chances: Peter, Jonah, Mark, Samson, David, and others. All trophies of God's grace."

Chrissy smiled as she listened to Poolee's sermon.

Just as God was patient and forgiving, she understood that God wanted the same of her. He had given her a second chance, another chance. She also had a clearer understanding that forgiveness was not the same as reconciliation. Forgiveness was between God's heart and hers, removing any barriers brought on by unforgiveness.

She had forgiven Jessie Belle, and while she did not care for Reina, she prayed for the woman who could be her twin sister. She also prayed for Traynor and his family, not yet able to accept the fact that they were her family, too.

Chrissy felt like a weight was lifted off her. She felt lighter than she had felt in years.

I'm finally free.

She was smart enough to know that this feeling was fleeting. Life was never perfect or without its share of problems, but Chrissy was okay.

She had something she had never had before—hope.

When Pastor Poolee finished his sermon, Chrissy slipped out of the sanctuary to change clothes. She was getting baptized this day.

She had already changed her clothes when she heard a knock and then Sabrina opened the door. "Ready?" she asked, a huge smile on her face.

"I am."

The two women embraced tightly.

"I'm so happy for you, Chrissy."

Chrissy smiled. "Thank you for showing me the way."

Sabrina led the way back into the sanctuary.

Pastor Poolee waited for Chrissy as she walked down the three steps into the baptistery. He took her hands and helped her wade to the center.

She cupped her hand and prepared to hold her nose.

"I baptize you in the name of the Father, and of the Son, and of the Holy Spirit," Pastor Poolee said as he lowered her under the water.

When she came back up, Chrissy was overcome by emotion. "Thank you, Lord," she yelled. "Thank You for loving me when I didn't love myself…thank You. I give my life over to you…"

Sabrina was there to wrap a towel around her., "That's it. Give it over to Him."

For the first time, Chrissy did just that.

Chapter 23
Six months later

Natalia floated down the aisle on her uncle's arm toward the man she would love forever. Tears flowed freely as she gazed at Dean. She couldn't wait to be his wife.

They stood facing each other as they said their vows.

Natalia spoke first. "Dean, you are my one true love, and I take you to be my husband. I will cherish our union and love you more each day than I did the day before. I promise to trust and respect you, laugh and cry with you. I promise to love you faithfully through good times and bad, regardless of the obstacles we may face together. I give you my hand, my heart, and my love completely, from this day forward for as long as we both shall live."

"Natalia, I love you and today I give myself to you in marriage. I know in my heart that God brought us together. I want you to know that I eagerly anticipate the chance to grow together. I promise to encourage and inspire you, to laugh with you, and to comfort you in times of sorrow and struggle. I promise to love and cherish you through whatever life may bring us. These things I give to you today, and all the days of our life."

His words brought more tears to her eyes.

Dean pulled a handkerchief out of his pocket and gently dabbed at her eyes.

Natalia was a basket of emotions as she waited to hear the words that would make their union real to her and all of the wedding guests.

"I now pronounce you man and wife ..."

She exhaled a long sigh of pleasure.

Natalia felt like she had been waiting a very long time to hear those words, but in reality it had only been almost nine months since she met him. Three months later, they were engaged.

Dean pulled Natalia into his arms, drawing her close. He pressed his lips to hers for a chaste, yet meaningful kiss.

Grinning, Dean escorted his bride down the aisle and through the double exit doors at the back of the church. They escaped into a nearby room waiting until it was time to go back into the chapel for the wedding photographs.

His eyes traveled down the length of her, nodding in obvious approval. "You look so beautiful, sweetheart."

Natalia broke into a big smile. "We're married." She held up her left hand to show off the stunning wedding set. "I can truly say that this is the happiest day of my life."

Sabrina, who had served as Maid of Honor, walked

over to them.

"Congratulations. To God be the glory." She hugged Natalia. "I love seeing you so happy, cousin."

"God knew what He was doing when that house burned down," she responded. "It brought us together, Sabrina."

"I love you."

Natalia smiled. "I love you, too."

Chrissy walked into the room. "It's a done deal."

Dean laughed and agreed. "She can't change her mind now."

"I have no plans of changing my mind," Natalia stated. "You are mine, honey."

The bridal party returned into the sanctuary for formal wedding photos and right after that, they headed over to the reception.

Natalia and Dean Anderson strolled hand in hand around the room, greeting their guests.

She broke into a smile when she saw Traynor. "I'm so glad that you decided to come."

He hugged her. "Thank you for inviting me to witness such a beautiful union."

She embraced Mary Ellen who whispered, "This is the woman I remember."

Warmth filled her. "Thank you for coming."

Their wedding menu consisted of chicken stuffed with crabmeat, seared pork tenderloin, mixed vegetables, brown rice and an assortment of rolls. Natalia's gaze navigated the room, checking to see if her guests were enjoying the meal that it had taken her weeks to plan.

"Everything is perfect," Dean whispered as if to reassure her.

"You know me so well."

He kissed her.

The room erupted into applause.

Natalie looked at her handsome husband and laughed. The only thing that could have made this day any more perfect was if her parents were in attendance. It gave her peace to know that they were with her in spirit.

She knew that God brought her and Dean together—she was sure of it. He knew who was right for her. Natalie raised her eyes heavenward, sending up silent words of gratitude.

After they finished eating, the bride and groom stood up and headed to the middle of the room to dance for the first time as husband and wife.

Natalia was looking forward to this dance and to spending the rest of her life with this wonderful man.

****

Chrissy watched the happy couple as they glided around the room talking to their guests. She never once thought she would ever be in a good place emotionally and physically. Her life had certainly changed for the better since giving her life to Christ.

Living with Sabrina and Natalia had been a wonderful experience, but she was glad to be in her own apartment.

She was now a real estate broker and doing well financially.

"She looks really happy," Sabrina said, referring to Natalia.

Chrissy agreed. "She does."

Sabrina stole a quick peek across her shoulder to where he sat. "Traynor's here."

"I know," she responded. "I spoke to him earlier."

"Don't you want to get to know your family, Chris?"

"I do," she admitted. "But they have been through so much already, Sabrina. I really don't want to be a part of that."

"They may not see this as a negative."

"I'm not sure Holt is going to want anything to do with me. Especially once he finds out that I'm the one who hurt his mother."

"Chris, you didn't know you had a mental disorder at the time and you weren't on medication. That's all changed, sweetie."

She thought about Sabrina's words for a moment. "I wanted to know who my birth mother was and I have that answer. I'm satisfied."

She could tell that Sabrina wasn't convinced.

"I'm fine with the way things are," she reiterated. "When the time is right, Holt and I will meet."

"You also have a little nephew and twin nieces to meet as well."

Chrissy smiled. "I have to admit that I can hardly wait to see them."

"Just don't wait until they're in college."

She laughed. "I won't, Sabrina."

One of the groomsmen walked over to Chrissy and asked, "Would you like to dance?"

She looked up at him and smiled. "Certainly."

Chrissy pushed away from the table and stood up.

He took her by the hand. "C'mon beautiful."

She felt a warm glow flow through her. Chrissy felt a bottomless peace and satisfaction.

God loved her and because of His love, she was a better person. She had learned to love herself.

When the dance ended, Chrissy straightened herself with dignity and allowed her partner to escort her back to her table.

****

Reina slipped on a pair of dark sunglasses as she made her way through the London airport. She had cut off her honey blond curls, dyed her hair a soft brown color that complemented her dark brown contacts.

Six months in Mexico had been great, but it was time for her to move on. As much as Reina wanted to focus on her future, some things had to be settled before she could move on.

Disappointment still filled her to the core that Traynor of all people did not embrace her—after all, she was the daughter of his beloved Jessie Belle. She was tired of people letting her down. Why couldn't Holt and

Traynor understand—why didn't they realize that everything she had done was for them?

She shrugged off her turbulent feelings.

No looking back, Reina promised herself.

She was starting over with a new plan in mind. She planned to take her time and consider every possible scenario before making a move. For now, she would wait, but Reina was determined to have the family she always wanted, always deserved.

One day, she would go back to Raleigh, and Reina vowed that her return would mean torment for the Deveraux family and anyone else who got in her way. Images of Mary Ellen and Natalia entered her mind. Those two in particular were definitely going to pay for interfering in her life. They would pay dearly.

"Miss Bell …"

She turned around. "Yes."

"I'm Chris… your driver. If you give me your claim tickets, I'll retrieve your luggage."

Running her fingers through her short hair, she broke into a smile. "Thank you, Chris. There is no need to be so formal. Just call me Jessie."

She would have her revenge.

Jezebel's Saga Continues in….

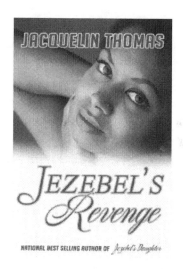

Coming Fall 2015….

Preorder Your Copy Today at

www.BrownGirlsBooks.com

ABOUT THE AUTHOR

Jacquelin Thomas has published over 69 books in the romance, women's fiction, and young adult genres. When she is not writing, Jacquelin enjoys spending time with her family, decorating and shopping. Jacquelin can be reached at: jacquelinthomas@yahoo.com.

Made in the USA
Middletown, DE
12 September 2015